Endles

a
RUSH
novella

Emma Scott

Cover design by First Edition Design Publishing

Ebook formatting by That Formatting Lady

Acknowledgments

A huge thank you to my beta readers, Erin Thomasson Cannon and Priscilla Perez. Erin, you never fail to boost me up when and I need it, and Priscilla, you're like a gift dropped from the sky. Thank you, both.

Thank you to Kathleen Ripley for her editing services, though all lingering mistakes are mine (because I can't help but go back in and mess around after she's done).

Thanks too, to Angela Shockley, my formatter, who saved my butt from my oncoming deadline, and whose patience with my endless changes is so very appreciated.

And a tremendous thank you to Michele Miesner, a RUSH reader who said to me, "You should write Noah's memoir!" The seed was planted and wouldn't stop growing. This book wouldn't exist if not for you. <3

Dedication

⠙⠑⠙⠊⠉⠁⠞⠊⠕⠝

    This book is dedicated to the generous, kind, amazing readers of
RUSH. You have warmed my heart with countless expressions of how
much Noah and Charlotte's love story meant to you. As a writer, there is
nothing more gratifying than to know my words have touched someone
or made them feel something strong, or that my characters have stayed
with them long after the story ends. This novella is my thank you to you,
for giving me such a tremendous gift.

                            Thank you.

Endless Possibility

a RUSH novella

Prologue

⠏⠗⠕⠇⠕⠛⠥⠑

Lenox Hill Hospital, February

Charlotte

My footsteps echo down the wide, linoleum hallway to join the sounds of machines and voices, hushed at this late hour, but still loud in my ears. Hospitals are not restful places, and the air is humid with disinfectant and tears. I hate it. I hate that he's here again. *It's not fair. He's already paid his dues, a million times over.*

I wasn't supposed to be here either; visiting hours are long over, but the nursing staff is lenient with me. Or they don't want a scene. Probably the latter.

The sign on the wall says 8C. His room. I heave a deep breath, to infuse my voice with strength to take the tremor out. Otherwise Noah will know immediately how scared I am. He's scared too. He tries not to show it; to push it down and bury it, but I know he is. I know *him.*

It's late, but Noah's awake, his eyes open and focused on nothing. He looks weak and pale beneath the covers, and too many tubes and lines are coming out of his arms. Too many machines monitoring the air in his lungs; his temperature and his heartbeat.

I have his heart, I think fiercely. *His and mine, they beat together.*

Noah turns his head as I step inside, and a smile finds its way to his lips. He can always tell when it's me.

"Hi, baby," he says tiredly. "What time is it?"

"Almost eleven." I cross the room to his side and drop my heavy bag at my feet. "Lucien has taken everyone home, but they'll be back first thing in the morning. Ava too."

"Ava's flying in?" he asks, a grimace flits over his face. "God, what a mess."

I kiss my fingers and touch it to the line between his dark brows. "They're your family. Nothing would keep them away, and that's how it should be."

He doesn't say anything but I know he's beating himself up. As if it's his fault the migraines have been relentless. Or that he collapsed yesterday afternoon like a puppet with its strings cut.

He reaches for my hand. "What about you? Go home, baby. Get

some sleep."

"Like hell," I say lightly, kicking off my shoes.

"Aren't visiting hours over?"

"They don't apply to me."

He manages a smile. "I can only imagine what would happen if they try to kick you out."

"Not gonna happen. Scoot. You're hogging the bed."

I lay down beside him, one jeans-clad leg thrown over his that are under the blankets. We lay face to face, our fingers entwined, our bodies touching as much as the narrow bed allows.

"Charlotte, you're trembling."

"It's cold in here. It's so cold in hospitals, have you noticed that?"

He shakes his head slightly against the pillow. "I'm sorry, baby. I never wanted to scare you. It's why I never said anything. Or maybe I was trying not to scare myself. I thought if I admitted how bad it was, I'd make it real." He laughs dryly. Darkly. "And yeah, I was right. It all feels pretty fucking real."

He squeezes his eyes shut as if his head pains him with yet another migraine. He'd had so many in the last few months; more than I could count. More than he was willing to tell me. Enough to alarm the doctors who'd ordered a barrage of tests today: CT scans, MRIs and even an X-ray, 'just to be safe,' on top of a million blood tests, until I thought they'd drained Noah dry.

The fear that those tests are going to turn up something bad has woven itself around all of us who love Noah best, and bound us tight. Something that would require more surgery, another craniotomy, maybe. Just thinking the word made me shiver.

Or maybe it was something worse. There were worse words, after all. Aneurism. Brain lesion. Tumor. And looming over all, the terrible specter of a word I couldn't even bring myself to *think*; that insidious, greedy thief that steals so much from this world and is never satisfied.

"I don't blame you for being scared, Noah," I say. "No one does."

"Yeah, well, I should have said something sooner but I didn't want to come back here. I thought I was done."

"I know." I press his fingers to my lips. "But this time it's different. You're going to be fine."

He nods and we both know that my words are just nothing more than hopeful wishing.

"I have some good news about your book," I say brightly. "Yuri couriered a printed manuscript over. So you can hold it. Feel the weight of *your* book in your hands."

Noah frowns. "It isn't even finished yet."

"I think it's his way of encouraging you." I give his arm a squeeze. "It's exciting. Len Gordon really wants it! Of course, I'd be *more* excited had you let me read it, *ever*—"

"It's not finished yet," Noah says again, and I jerk my gaze to him. He's not excited or thrilled, but looks angry. Or fearful. Or both, each emotion vying for center stage. "I wanted to finish it before you read it. Before anyone read it. But it doesn't have an ending." His hazel eyes search for me, his hands holding mine clench tighter. "I can't see the ending, Charlotte. What is it going to be?"

"Happy," I say. I *declare*. "It's going to be a happy ending, Noah."

He closes his eyes, ending their fruitless search. "I'm so tired, baby. I want to sleep now."

I nod, and kiss his lips. "Of course," I say, though I want him to keep talking to me until he feels better, but I realize, with a dull pang, I have nothing to say. No way to help him.

He slips away to what I hope will be a restful sleep, unbroken by pain, and I lie beside him, watching over him, our hands entwined. I struggle to keep my thoughts away from the What Ifs; the myriad things that might come out of the doctor's mouth when morning comes.

But the desire to help Noah is strong and makes me restless. Noah is sleeping and I need to let him, but I need to hear him too. To know his thoughts, to hold as much of him close to me as I can, in this dark hour.

I look to my bag, to where his book lies. He didn't want me to read it until it was finished, but I have to. I have to know how we got to this place, and why he kept his pain from me. I had to know what happened to him in Europe. He made peace with his blindness, but *how* he came to that was a long, arduous journey that took its toll on him. I wanted—no, *needed*—to know what he gave up and suffered for me. For us.

I carefully disentangle myself from him, and slip off the bed. I take the manuscript out of my bag, and sink into the chair by the window. The book is thin, not more than one hundred pages, bound in thick paper, punched three times with those brass page fasteners. I open the book to the opening page, still in its rough, unpolished fonts and format.

Endless Possibility
A memoir

Noah Lake

Dedication

For Lucien.
The god of my dark universe who said, "Let there be light," and so there was…

Charlotte
The light in my darkness. The reason I live instead of exist. You are the dawn of my every new day.
My endless possibility.

I blink away tears at these words, and turn to the first chapter.

I read about Noah's first loves: adrenaline, speed, fear. I read of some of his exploits with *Planet X,* and of his ingrained wanderlust, to never stop traveling and experiencing the world in all its splendor. I read of the events prior to his accident and then the accident itself; a harrowing descent into pain and darkness. I'm horrified to discover his recovery was so much worse than I'd ever known; so much more vivid in his own words than the awful Google photos of his injury I had seen. More terrible words like craniotomy and cerebral spinal fluid; shunts and screws, grafts that turned septic…And pain. So much pain. My love endured so much pain, I can hardly fathom it.

With tears blurring the pages, I read Noah's description of the day he was told the blindness was permanent; a heartbreaking list of experiences and places and people he'd never see, including the faces of his own children.

I read of his rehab and the amazing care of his therapist, a wise man named Harlan Williams—a man I instantly wanted to track down and hug for how he took care of my Noah through the worst of his grief.

I read of Noah's lonely, hopeless retreat to the townhouse here in New York, and of his succession of assistants whom he sought to drive away as he had his family.

And then I read about myself, of the day we met face-to-face, and here is Noah writing about hope and the start of something new and good. Us. Our messy, beautiful, up-and-down love that began with a job interview he didn't want to give with a young woman who needed only a little bit of security and peace to rest her bruised heart.

I read on, until I came to what I was looking for when I picked up the manuscript in the first place: the place where Noah and I were broken apart, so that he could undertake what he thought of as the quest to put us—and himself—back together.

This was the part of our story I didn't know, and this was what I needed to read: what happened to him in Europe and after; why he drove himself to the brink, and how he still didn't feel as if it were enough.

I'm scared for what I'm about to read, as this is *my* journey into the black unknown.

With a shaking breath, I turn the page, and plunge in.

New York City

⠝⠽⠉

I left her.

Just writing the words now, weeks later, still punches me in the gut. I left Charlotte and it was the worst thing and the best thing I had ever done.

The party at *Planet X* had been a disaster, just as she'd tried to warn me it would be. The humiliation of wandering the ballroom alone, a castaway with nothing to buoy me and no ability to see the shore was survivable. But Deacon McCormick trapped my Charlotte in an elevator and tried to force himself on her. That was unforgivable.

I didn't say a word at the police station while Charlotte relayed what happened, but on the inside I was screaming. Deacon had grabbed her chin, had tried to pry her mouth open to worm his tongue inside until she'd used the pepper spray my sister had given her.

My knuckles ached where I'd struck Deacon when he and Charlotte had spilled out of the poisoned elevator, and so I concentrated on that during the police statement, to try to keep from going mad with rage. I flexed my fingers mercilessly, savoring the pain. But those bones should have been broken. My hand didn't hurt enough. I hadn't hit him *hard enough*. I listened to the fear and humiliation in Charlotte's voice as she relayed what happened, and I wanted to kill Deacon. I wasn't a violent guy, but at that moment, had he been in front of me, I would have beat him until it was me they were throwing in jail.

That incident showed me how far away I was from being capable of giving Charlotte the life she deserved. My stupidity and pride had put her in the worst of situations. The anger and bitterness were still there, lurking beneath the surface. My fruitless desire to have things go back to the way they were, to pick up my life where it left off, was as potent as ever...a poison that was seeping between Charlotte and me, and ruining us. I had to leave.

I had no plan. We got back to the townhouse and I immediately went to my room and began packing, grabbing clothes at random. I needed to get out quickly, before I could change my mind.

Charlotte brought me my sunglasses and cane—from Valentina of all people—and I was wracked all over again. Thanks to Deacon's lies, Val had kissed me, and Charlotte had probably seen that too.

"What are you doing?" Charlotte asked, her voice breaking and filling with tears.

Saving us, I wanted to say, but that sounded too heroic, and I was anything but. I was trying to outrun the humiliation of my own failure. I'd had many that night, but above all, I had failed to protect Charlotte. Deacon, I realized, had hit me much harder than I had hit him. He hit me where it hurt the most, and Charlotte had almost paid the worst price.

It was time to go. She cried and I held her, felt her clutching my shirt, heard her tears and pain. I asked her to wait for me. I didn't even know what I was saying, what I was asking. Wait for what? For me to get my shit together, I supposed, though I hadn't the first idea how. But I'd been a selfish ass for months, and this was the first thing I'd done that felt like giving back. It felt horrible and heartbreaking, but there was nothing left for me to do.

"I love you, Charlotte," I told her. For the first time. Telling her as I left her. Leaving because I loved her. "I love you more than my own self and that's the only reason I can walk out that door tonight."

I kissed her then, to taste and feel her one last time, but also to silence her. If she told me not to go, I'd have given in. The pain in my heart was a lead weight. Collapsing to my knees and begging her forgiveness would've been so much easier. And wrong.

So I kissed her quickly and left her, and shut the door behind me.

I stepped onto the sidewalk in the early morning hours. It was still quiet; the air felt thick with humidity, maybe rain. I dug my white stick out of the luggage and tapped my way down the sidewalk until I felt the curve of the curb. I rounded the corner, out of sight of the townhouse should Charlotte think to come after me, and fished my cell phone from my pocket. I'd told her I'd called a cab, but that was a lie. I had no plan, no idea what to do next. I told my phone to call Lucien.

I was still wearing a tux, for Christ's sake, though I'd long ago torn off the bow. I ripped the top three buttons of my shirt open as I waited for the call to go through, feeling like I was suffocating. Lucien's sleep-thickened voice answered.

"Allo? Noah?"

So much concern. And I'd treated him so badly. This man, who'd been like a second father to me. Who'd put up with me, who hired assistants for me while I systematically fired them or drove them away. But for one. He'd brought me Charlotte, and had I ruined that too? All the bullshit I'd barricaded myself behind was falling away, leaving me naked and exposed out there on the street. Lost.

"Lucien," I croaked, my voice sounding as broken down and raw as I felt. I said something I hadn't said to anyone since the accident. "I need you."

I hadn't been to Lucien's high-rise condo in a decade. I vaguely remembered tasteful art—mostly glass sculptures and Waterford crystal—and the smell of his Dunhill cigarettes. As he led me inside, the scent of that smoke and his expensive cologne were like a shot of nostalgia in the arm. He sat me down on a leather chair—if it was the same as I'd remembered, it was a deep green color—and lit a cigarette.

"So," Lucien said, exhaling. "Tell me."

"I left Charlotte."

"So I have observed. Why?"

"To save us."

From outside the windows, I felt the warmth of the sun on my arm and the sounds of the city coming back to life while I was dying inside. I told him everything that happened at the *Planet X* party, the words pouring out of my mouth—a torrent of shame I needed to let out before pride dammed it back.

I told Lucien how Charlotte had worked so tirelessly to show me a better life, and how I repaid her by leaving her alone with that bastard, Deacon.

"But she is safe now," Lucien said, his voice tinged with ice.

"Yes," I said. "Safely away from me. She has an audition next week for a touring orchestra. They go all over Europe, and I know she'll get in. She's too good not to."

"I was under the impression Charlotte felt out of touch with her music as of late. Since her brother passed?"

"She's getting it back. Finding it again. This tour…it's perfect for her. It's her time. I know it, and I think she does too. And she…she wanted me to go with her," I said, pain squeezing my heart. "But I can't tag along. I'd just drag her down. She's spent the last few months living for me. She needs to live for herself."

"And you don't think that's a determination she can make on her own?"

"Of course she can," I snapped. "And if I weren't fucked up, I'd do whatever she wanted. But I *am* fucked up—the party last night is proof enough. So I can't go with her and fuck that up too. She'd keep putting herself before me instead of concentrating on her music. And tour or no tour, I have to figure out how to live. If I can't do that...I'm not good for her. Not how I am."

Silence.

I shifted irritably. Admitting to screwing up is hard enough. It's a million times worse when you can't see the face of the person you're admitting it to. I felt like a blindfolded captive waiting for the axe to fall. Or not.

Finally, Lucien's chair creaked; I imagined he sat back, pondering, smoke wafting around his silver hair in lazy tendrils. "The question remains, then, what are you going to do? You told Charlotte to wait for you. Wait for what?"

"I don't know. I don't know what the fuck I'm doing." I rubbed my hands over my face. "Feel free to share any bright ideas."

"Noah," Lucien said, "even if I had an answer, it is for you to discover. But I would remind you that you have the love of an extraordinary young woman. Please remember that before you bury yourself in self-hatred."

Charlotte's words back at the police station came back to haunt me.

"Deacon backed me into the corner of the elevator. He...gripped my chin. Hard. To pry my mouth open..."

I shuddered. "Too late."

"Quoi?"

"Nothing."

I rubbed the back of my head where a soft glow of pain began to swell. Apparently the night wasn't done being monumentally shitty; the Monster was waking.

"Migraine?" Lucien's voice sounded sharper, jolted by concern.

I nodded and fished around in my tux jacket for my meds. Charlotte, of course, had thought to drop them into my pocket before we left for the party.

"I'm fucking hungover, too."

The air tightened with Lucien's surprise. "You drank?"

"Oh, yeah. I'm just full of bad decisions tonight."

I heard the chair squeak, footsteps over floorboards, and then a running faucet. Lucien returned and pressed a glass of water against my hand. I tossed back the Azapram, washed it down. Then his hand on my shoulder. "Come."

He led me to his guest room that smelled clean but unused. I sat on the bed and immediately realized how tired I was. The headache was sluggish, slow. I thought the drugs and sleep would catch it before it blew up, but I didn't care all that much. *Serve me right.*

"There is a bathroom across from the bed on the left," Lucien said. "After you've had a chance to rest, we'll talk and perhaps a solution to your predicament will make itself known."

"Lucien," I said before he shut the door. "Thank you."

"Of course, my boy. Sleep well."

He said it like a friend, and not like a man paid gobs of money by my father to take care of me, and that was the best goddamn thing to happen to me all night.

I slumped onto the bed. The pain in the back of my head slunk away, and I fell into nothing.

Book of Revelations

⠿ ⠿⠿ ⠿⠿⠿ ⠿⠿⠿⠿ ⠿⠿⠿⠿⠿

There are few things that remind you of a disastrous night more than waking up alone in a cold bed. I woke reaching for Charlotte. I reached across an empty space for her warmth, for her skin, and the softness of her hair. I wanted her lips on mine, smiling against my mouth as she told me "Good morning." I'd only been sharing a bed with her in the townhouse for little more than a week, but it had already begun to feel like life.

But she wasn't in the townhouse. *I* wasn't in the townhouse. It took me a moment to organize the scents and sounds of the room and remember it was Lucien's guest room in his Park Avenue condo. He was on the twenty-third floor and had a spectacular view of Central Park. I had been thirteen years old or so the last time I'd been here, and of course hadn't appreciated the view. Then, I'd wanted only to go higher.

Then, I'd thought I was invincible.

I sat up slowly. No migraine, but my mouth felt like I'd been eating dirt by the handful all night and my stomach wasn't happy about it. I felt my way around the wall until I found the bathroom door, then had to feel around for the goddamn toilet. I cursed myself for not visiting Lucien more often when I could see the fucking layout of his apartment. And his face. Lucien's appearance—the exact details—was slipping from my memory, like a sketch slowly erased. My parents too. And Ava. I had Charlotte but only because I touched her face so often. But now that she was gone; what if I lost that too?

The thought made me more nauseated than my hangover.

I took a piss that lasted approximately ten hours, and then fumbled my way toward the kitchen. Mercifully, Lucien heard me and led me to the breakfast table, while he poured me a cup of strong, black coffee.

"Hungry?" he asked. "It's well after lunch time."

I shook my head. "Am I keeping you from work?"

"Not at all."

Lucien, like my father, was semi-retired. He had an office on Wall Street, where he managed my father's money and real estate deals, and those of several other clients. But mostly for my dad. He was more family than employee, and now spent most of his time handling my parents' retirement. Since my accident, he'd been relegated to my handler; taking care of me after I'd evicted everyone else from my life.

Why him?

I don't know what it was about Lucien Caron, but he was the only person I could tolerate, even when in the grips of my blackest moods. There was something constant about him that soothed me, or maybe he was just impervious to my vitriol where everyone else had been driven away by it. And I sincerely hoped that that wasn't going to fade away too.

"And did you sleep well?" he asked now, his voice mild.

"I guess. I haven't woken up to any epiphany."

Lucien made a noise like *Hmm.* I heard the flick of a lighter and then the smell of smoke. "And Charlotte? Will you speak to her today?"

"No," I said. "That's the only thing I know to do. To stay away from her. To let her prepare for her audition without interference or distraction from me."

"Are you certain she will audition at all?"

"Yeah, she will. She's strong. And brave." I swallowed. "She'll do it and she'll get in. They'd be crazy not to give her a seat."

"Hmmm." An exhalation of smoke. "On that note, I have news regarding that transaction you asked me to make in Connecticut."

"You found a violin?" I asked. "Or did you sell the car?"

"Both, in a manner of speaking."

Three years before my accident, I bought a 1969 Camaro Z28 Tribute. Black with white racing stripes, monster block, and 450 horsepower after I'd souped it up. I had bought it needing some work, and after I'd spent a year on it, off and on, it was a masterpiece of engineering and speed. I had a buddy who let me drive it at Daytona once, and that had been one of the greatest thrills of my life.

The morning after Charlotte and I had been mugged, and her violin stolen, we went to meet my family in Connecticut. My sister, Ava, had given me an earful about what a lost instrument meant to a musician of Charlotte's caliber. That, plus Charlotte's own tearful confession that she felt like "an amputee" had spurred me to action.

"She needs something exceptional," I'd told Lucien, speaking in French in case Charlotte overheard. "But I'm not asking my parents for it. It's going to come from me, one hundred percent."

Lucien had been hesitant. "The type of violin you wish to purchase for Charlotte is cost prohibitive. You could drain your savings or draw from your 401(k), neither option I recommend. Or…"

"Or sell the Camaro."

"Oui."

I couldn't drive it. I couldn't even stash it somewhere and admire it. It was stowed in a garage in Miami, gathering dust. And yet, it hurt.

I'd spat the words before I could take them back. "Do it."

Now, I mentally prepared myself to hear him tell me the car was gone. It shouldn't have fucking mattered. It was for Charlotte after all, but it was quite literally the last remnant of my old life. An actual embodiment of the fast and dangerous lifestyle that was forever closed off to me.

"You found a buyer for the Camaro?"

"I did. The offer is quite generous, and the sale shall be finalized by the end of the week."

I waited to feel supremely shitty about that, but instead felt like a burden had been lifted.

This. This is the first step toward letting it all go. This moment, right here.

"The violin is another matter," Lucien was saying. "There is an auction at Christie's in The Hague for a Johannes Cuypers."

"A what?"

"A fine violin. Exceptional."

Exceptional. Exactly what Charlotte deserved. "Good. Get it."

Lucien chuckled. "Would it were that simple. But I shall do my best to secure it for her before her tour begins."

Business concluded, a silence fell between us. I could practically hear Lucien's smile slide off his face.

"Go ahead," I said. "Say it."

"And what is it I am to say?"

"You think I'm making a mistake? Or being an asshole, to leave her like I did?"

"You would know that better than I," Lucien replied evenly. "But am I concerned for her? Yes, of course."

"It's the best thing. And aren't you always telling me that the best thing is rarely the easiest?"

"I have been known to use that phrase from time to time."

"Well, this isn't easy. It's the hardest fucking thing I've ever done, so it has to be right."

"Your conviction is admirable," Lucien said, "but quite pointless if you haven't any direction. My support of your leaving Charlotte—a young lady whom I love and cherish as if she were my own—is tolerable so long as you do what you promised. So?" He clapped his hands.

"Allons-y. Braille classes? A seeing-eye dog? I'm quite certain there are facilities for the blind in which you can be taught how to live independently. Say the word, and I shall do or acquire anything you need."

"I…don't know." I turned my coffee mug around and around. "I'm willing to take classes, I guess. But…it doesn't feel right. Or enough. It doesn't feel like *me.*"

Lucien made a sound like hmmm, deep in his throat. "You need to find your epiphany, Noah," he said flatly. "And quickly. Charlotte is suffering from your departure, yes? And you are quite miserable without her."

"Miserable doesn't begin to cut it."

I heard a chair scrape; Lucien rose to his feet, his words rained down from on high. "Then it is imperative you answer the question, *What will you do?* with the right answer. And quickly, before it's too late."

Four days later, and I hadn't done a damn thing. My parents wanted to see me, but I had no desire to go to Connecticut and explain my *Planet X* failure to them, nor had I figured out my grand plan. I lay around, wracking my brain for a solution to my problem that didn't involve sitting behind a desk studying Braille, or learning cute fucking tricks for labeling food cans, or how to cook a meal without burning myself or the house down.

The afternoon of the fifth day, Lucien got the call. Charlotte formally tendered her resignation as my assistant. I wanted to fly at Lucien and grab the phone, to hear Charlotte's voice, even if it meant her cursing my name. But I glued myself to the couch with white-knuckled fists and listened. It was a short call, and when Lucian ended it, I heard him sigh.

"So?" I leaned forward. "She got it, right?"

"She did."

Fierce pride swept through me. "Good for you, baby," I murmured under my breath.

"She will be departing for Europe in four days," Lucien said.

My head shot up. "Four days? The violin won't make it in time."

"I thought of that," Lucien said. "Charlotte arrives in Vienna next

19

week but the tour doesn't begin for two weeks after that. It is quite possible that we'll have secured the violin by then, and can send it prior to her first concert on July 2nd."

"I wish I could just put it in her hands myself," I muttered. "I'm happy for her, but goddamn, she's going to be so far away."

"Yes," Lucien said. "Quite the whirlwind tour from what she told me. Seventeen cities in a month and a half."

"Which only proves my suspicion that had I gone with her, she'd spend all her time dragging my ass around instead of concentrating on her music."

"Mmmm."

"But I'd like to hear her play," I said, talking mostly to myself. "I'd really like that."

"I have taken the liberty of researching a facility that will help you live independently," Lucien was saying. "The Helen Keller Foundation. In Brooklyn. Quite reputable."

"Uh, what? Oh, yeah. Okay."

"Perhaps you could spend the summer studying, and then fly to Vienna to meet Charlotte on your own. Show her you have put the time and effort into fulfilling your promise by putting your newfound skills to the test."

"What? Alone?"

The idea seemed preposterous. And frightening. I'd spent the better portion of my adult-non-visually-impaired life navigating the world's cities and their airports. It was often a challenge as a sighted person. To do it blind? Impossible.

But as for the rest, I asked Charlotte to wait for me, but wait for what? And for how long? If I wasn't going to make the effort to learn how to live blind, why the fuck did I leave her?

I waved a hand. "Yeah, go ahead. Sign me up. Classes, Braille, all of it."

"Wonderful," Lucien said. "I will make the arrangements this minute."

I sighed. "Wonderful."

That evening, I lay in the guest bedroom, listening to Mozart's Violin

Concerto No. 5 on my phone when Lucien knocked.

"This arrived for you," he said, and I felt the bed dip. "It's the software Charlotte recommended. With it, you can read and write on a computer, and even go online and peruse the Internet. It will read the screen for you. Quite extraordinary technology!"

He sounded so excited about it. I managed a thin smile.

"Sounds great."

"Quite!" Lucien said. "And you're enrollment at the Helen Keller Foundation is complete. Classes begin next week, so there is time to squeeze in a visit to New Haven. Your parents are anxious to see you."

"Okay. Thanks."

"Noah?"

"Yeah?"

"I'm proud of you."

The door closed and I sank back down on the bed. He was proud. I was as conflicted as ever. Classes at the Helen Keller Foundation. Whoopee-fuckin'-doo. It still felt off to me, though I couldn't see I had any other option.

Back in the day, when I was still working for *Planet X* and some article wasn't coming together the way I wanted it to, I'd just start typing. Anything and everything about the subject I was working on, just off the top of my head. Riff writing, someone called it. And when I was done, I'd go in and pick all the best, truest parts and organize those into the article.

I needed that now. To be able to just spew all my feelings and thoughts about what it would take to fulfill my promise to Charlotte so I could analyze them. A jumble of words, maybe, but some of those would float to the top and I'd have my answer.

I called Lucien back into the room and asked him to set up the software Charlotte sent me on his laptop, as mine was still in the townhouse. Lucien was pushing seventy-five, but he was still sharp as a whip. He got it up and running, and showed me how to speak into it, and how to have that read back to me. Then left me to it.

I toyed with the mic for a good ten minutes, feeling supremely stupid. But the question needed answering.

You want to learn how to live blind? Then fucking learn, snowflake. There is no other way.

Except that wasn't what I wanted. I didn't *want* to learn to function blind. I didn't want to be blind at all. My grief wasn't deep or poetic. It was sinister in its simplicity. I wanted to see again and I never would. That was my torment: two implacable forces, smashing up against one another like tectonic plates along a fault, waiting for the other to give. My blindness couldn't and I didn't want to, so I remained caught between them. And it was crushing the life out of me.

"I don't want to be blind," I said aloud.

Tell us something we don't know, genius.

Apparently, my inner editor had become an asshole since the accident.

But it was the crux of the problem. It *was* the problem. I didn't want to be blind. I wished I'd never fucking jumped off that cliff. Or that I had jumped at the right time, or a different time and suffered a different injury. Something that wasn't so goddamn life-altering.

Without realizing it, I began to speak, soothing my bitter anguish with an alternate reality. A fantasy of what might've been…

I dove too late. I know it even as my feet leave the rocky outcropping. I have time enough to think 'This is going to end badly' and then I'm in the water, curving into the dive. The water tosses me and I slam against the rocks. Pain explodes up my right side. It feels as if a giant steel trap has snapped over my leg from ankle to hip. Or maybe a shark bit me. The pain is both the deep agony of shattering bone and the burning fire of torn flesh. Panicked, I nearly inhale ocean water as I claw my way to the surface.

Local divers haul me to the shore. I suck in deep breaths to calm myself and then nearly lose it all over again to see my right leg. It's a fucking horror show, there's no other way to put it. Bent and twisted, skin torn away, it looks like I have three knees instead of one, and blood is seeping into the sand. The sun is hot on my damp skin, but I begin to shiver.

An ambulance arrives and I'm whisked to the naval hospital, then airlifted to UCLA Medical Center the next day. Three surgeries later, I wake up to Lucien and my parents around me, all of them trying really hard not to look at my leg. I don't want to look at it. It's caged in metal scaffolding from my ankle to just above my right knee. Steel pins from the scaffold penetrate my bloated, bruised skin in eight different places, holding my bones in place, though I have more titanium rods than bones now.

I want to vomit, but the doctors tell me that while it looks godawful, I'll be able to walk and run and live a normal life again, given time and a shit-ton of rehab.

"It could've been worse," they tell me over and over.

It could've been worse. A-fucking-men.

When I'm able, they fly me to Lenox Hill Hospital in New York City for another few weeks, until the pins come out. My imprisoned leg is free, and then I head to White Plains for physical therapy. My therapist is a great guy named Harlan Williams. We talk and joke around—nothing serious—as I work to get my leg back to where it was.

Two weeks later, I'm in an ankle-to-hip leg brace and hobbling around on crutches. The brace can't come off for another six weeks, so my parents lend me their townhouse in New York City and Lucien hires me an assistant to help me out around the house. Some guy named Trevor. He's okay, but I don't give him much to do. I want to regain my independence as fast as I can and get back out there for *Planet X.* Yuri, my editor, is griping that he needs me back and I'm more than happy to oblige.

But I still need to recuperate, and I'm bored as hell cooped up in the townhouse. Some buddies of mine from PX stop by and we head out to a brunch place on Amsterdam Street my assistant sometimes orders from.

Deacon, Logan, Polly, Jonesy and I take a table in Annabelle's Bistro, and settle in for a good two hours, running our waitress ragged. She's a cute little brunette doing her best to stay cheerful for us while we give her a hard time with endless coffee refills, loud laughter, swearing, and general obnoxiousness.

Her nametag says Charlotte, and Deacon calls her *"Sweet Charlotte"* and ogles and teases her, sometimes inappropriately. She has pretty eyes, I muse, but otherwise pay her no mind. I have my leg up on a chair in the corner, leaning back, as if I haven't a care in the world. And I don't. I'm going to make a full recovery and pick up my life right where I left off.

Finally, a manager with a severe hairdo and too much makeup, politely, yet pointedly, inquires if there's anything else we need, and we take the hint. We gather our shit and Deacon picks up the tab. We file out, through the maze of tables, and I'm last, hobbling slowly on crutches.

I'm halfway out when I realize I left my Yankees baseball cap on the table. I return to get it and find the waitress staring at the check with tears in her eyes. She snaps the black leather book shut when she sees me and hurriedly turns away.

"Forget something?" she asks with false cheer and a shaky smile.

"My hat," I say. She's short and I'm tall. I tower over her. *"Did*

Deacon leave a shitty tip? He does that."

"Oh no, no, I mean...it's fine," she says, turning away to wipe her eyes. "I'm so sorry. I just...um, kind of a rough month. You know how it is." She glances me up and down in my expensive jeans and designer shirt. "Or maybe you don't."

The waitress realizes what she said, and another round of apologies bursts out of her as she begins stacking our dirty dishes. "Oh my god, I'm so sorry. Really. I have this bad habit...blurting. I don't know why I said that. Anyway, um..."

I laugh, and fish into my back pocket for my wallet. "Don't worry about it. And take this. For your trouble."

I offer her forty dollars and her eyes widen. Up close, her eyes are even prettier—large and luminous, but sad too.

A blush turns her skin scarlet "Oh, no, I couldn't. No, please. It's fine, really." She bustles even faster now, not looking at me.

I shrug and drop the twenties on the table. "I hope your month improves."

She stops and stares at the money, at war with herself.

"Okay. Thank you," she says finally, her voice cracking. She takes the money and stuffs it into her apron.

I feel sorta bad, poor girl.

"Have a nice day, Charlotte," I say, and start to hobble away.

She calls after me, "I hope your leg gets better soon."

That was big of her, considering what ginormous bastards we'd been to her all morning. Or maybe she's just doing her job.

I wave a hand to her without looking back, and leave Annabelle's.

Time heals me. I go back to work. To Planet X. To the world and all its thrills and beauty. I don't go back to my parents' townhouse; hell I'm hardly in NYC anymore. I don't go back to Annabelle's and I never see—or think about—that cute waitress with the sad eyes ever again.

"Fucking hell," I whisper as the machine reads the last line of what I'd 'written.'

I feel sick. Disgusted. *Terrified.* My own imagination took my 'just a broken leg' fantasy and carried it on a terrible tide to a fucking terrible conclusion.

When my nerves stop jangling, and I'm able to pull myself away from the awfulness of that manufactured alternate reality, clarity hits me like a breath of fresh air.

I knew what I needed to do. I needed to live up to my promise to

Charlotte, but spending a sweltering summer in a classroom in Brooklyn, trapped behind a desk and thousands of miles away from her wasn't the way to do it. I wasn't sedentary. I was a world-traveler and always had been. Now that my ass was out of the townhouse—thanks to her—moving slowly was better than not moving at all.

I had to keep moving. Always. To her. She was at the end of a long, dark road where I was going to be beset with impossible obstacles, and maybe even danger, but I had to make that journey. I had to do everything possible for Charlotte. Everything and anything.

Because the idea of failure, of living without her in my life, was a nightmare worse than blindness.

Preparing to Launch

Lucien and I went to my parents' house in New Haven and I told them my grand plan: to follow Charlotte's tour through Europe—without her knowledge—on my own. Naturally, they thought I was insane and my father was about ready to disown me for worrying my mother. Lucien wasn't happy either, but he managed to soothe my parents. Only Ava, of all people, thought I was doing the right thing.

"It's not stalking, is it?" I asked over the phone. "I mean, will she think I'm some sort of creepy asshole for following her around...?"

"Hiding in the bushes outside her hotel room?" Ava laughed.

"Something like that."

"She's more likely to be upset you were there the whole time and she couldn't be with you," my sister said, serious now.

"I'll have to take my chances that she'll hear me out when it's over and forgive me."

"She loves you. She'll forgive you."

"Would you?"

"I would," Ava said, "if it worked."

I felt second thoughts trying to creep in. What if traipsing blind around Europe alone didn't slay the demons that plagued me? More likely, the trek would wear them down until they croaked of exhaustion. Just the idea of navigating one city alone—never mind seventeen—made me want to lie down and pull the covers over my damn head until the whole crazy idea went away.

"It has to work," I said to Ava. "I have nothing else."

"Then go for it," she replied. "But Noah? Be fucking careful. I mean it. London is only a short flight to anywhere in Europe. You call me if shit gets dangerous or weird. Or hell, come home if it's too much. Okay?"

"Okay," I lied. I didn't know if my crazy plan was going to work, but I knew—with total certainty—that giving up was out of the question. And certainty, as my old buddy Harlan used to say, is its own kind of peace.

The eve of Charlotte's departure to Vienna arrived.

Call her, you asshole, I told myself. *If you let her leave without saying goodbye, you just might fuck it all up before it's even begun.*

I reached for my phone and the words "Call Charlotte" were on my lips, when my phone rang, announcing her call. I inhaled and let it out slowly, willing my heart to stop pounding against my ribs.

"Hi, babe."

"Hi," she said. "I'm sorry to call you so late. Or at all. I didn't know if you wanted to talk to me…"

I squeezed my eyes shut. She sounded so unsure, her voice full of tears and longing. But it felt so good to hear her again.

"Of course, I do," I said. "I've wanted to talk to you every day the last few days. But I was afraid to make it harder on us."

"It's already too hard."

"I know." I inhaled sharply. "Lucien told me about your audition. That's incredible and yet I'm not surprised at all. I'm so proud of you."

"I leave tomorrow," she said. "Did Lucien tell you that too?"

She was crying. Christ, I couldn't do it. It was all wrong, I was ruining us, and a thousand other thoughts like it flashed through me in a moment.

"Don't cry, baby. Please don't cry."

"I don't have much say in the matter. Noah, is this the right thing? Because it feels awful."

"It is. Please trust me." My throat started to close on me. I coughed. "Lucien is going to take you to the airport tomorrow. He'll meet you at the townhouse around eleven."

"And where will you be?"

"Wishing I was there, to kiss you and hold you one last time before you go. I love you."

"I love you too," she whispered. "I love you, Noah. I do."

I held the phone so tightly, I thought it'd shatter. I had to marshal my will or break down right then and there. "Have a safe flight, Charlotte," I managed, and hung up.

The phone slipped to the floor as I held my head in my hands. I sat that way for a long time.

The next day, I sat in my father's study, writing on my own laptop. I had begun what I thought of as a prologue. A prologue to what, I didn't know. I had the vague idea that I would document my trip across Europe as I went. Like the crazy-ass journey itself, writing about it felt right, even if I couldn't imagine how it would all play out in the end.

Lucien returned from taking Charlotte to the airport. Jealousy churned in my gut that he got to see her, talk to her, hug her goodbye.

"Did she make it through okay?"

"Yes, yes," he said. I heard him lower himself into the chair across from the desk. "She made it fine."

"How did she look?"

"Lovely, bien sûr," Lucien replied. "Are you quite certain that you wish to do this?"

I barked a short laugh. "Hell no. But you know what's at stake. You just took her to the airport."

Lucien made a noise but I could hear he was smiling. "Indeed. And I have good news. You had the winning bid for the Cuypers violin."

I smiled in what felt like the first time in eons, since I'd left Charlotte. "Really? Hot damn. How much?"

"$42,000. The Camaro sold for $47,600, which left you just enough to pay for insurance and special shipping and handling to Vienna."

I sat back, relief washing through me. "And it's a good one, right? The violin?"

I heard Lucien's smile color his words. "The best. Or, at the very least, the best in your price range."

Because that's what Charlotte deserved. The best violin I could afford, and the best version of me when all was said and done.

Auf Wiedersehen

At JFK, Lucien waited with me at my gate. He was allowed a special dispensation from security to accompany me until the plane took off. We sat side by side in the business class lounge of Austrian Airlines, he sipping champagne, me a bottle of water.

"If you recall," he said, amused, "I suggested you try to navigate *one* city alone."

"Go big or go home," I said, grinning like an idiot. I felt good. Optimistic. Naively unaware of the shit storm that awaited me. "You told me to answer the question, so I did. This is what I'm meant to do."

"I know. I'm worried about you to the marrow of my old bones, but I also know how this is right for you." Lucien chuckled. "Nothing has changed. You're still the daredevil you've always been and I wouldn't change you for all the tea in China."

I eased a sigh. "Thank you. That means a lot to me, Lucien. *You* mean a lot to me, though I know I haven't told you that enough."

"Noah! I hadn't pegged you as the sentimental sort."

"Blame Charlotte for that."

"Hmm, I believe I will thank her instead."

They called my flight, and we rose, Lucien guiding me to the queue to get on. I felt him studying me.

"Second thoughts?" he asked softly.

"A million of them. But that's not it." I hesitated. "I'm...I don't remember what people look like anymore. Mom and Dad...They're like blurred photos. And Ava. I know she's beautiful and that's all that sticks. And you. I can't remember you, Lucien."

"It's all right, my boy. I'm quite past my prime," he said, trying to be light while I was suddenly stricken with a glut of emotion. A dam— one of hundreds within me—began to crack.

I turned to Lucien, and before I could second guess myself or worry what other people thought, I put my hands on his face and looked at him....and he came back. All of him; his kind eyes, heavy brow, and a face drawn with laugh lines.

"Thank you for everything," I said thickly, and then cast off from the safety of him, into the black unknown.

Vienna
⠧⠊⠑⠝⠝⠁

It's pretty sad when the *flight* is the best part of your European tour.
Granted, I knew that this wasn't going to be a fucking picnic, but I wasn't
prepared for how utterly *unprepared* I actually was. I slept through the
flight and woke with hope and optimism. I mentally geared myself up for
the whole ordeal, as I used to do before a big jump or stunt back in my
old *PX* days. And it worked…until we landed.

The plane taxied, stopped, and then people started their mad
exodus to get off. I was in business class, but that didn't stop my fellow
travellers from acting as if there was a contest to see who could stand up,
gather their carry-ons, and then stand there waiting for the doors to open
the longest. I was walled-off by legs and carry-on bags.

I sat, unmoving in my seat, my guts twisting into knots, until it
sounded like the plane was nearly empty. A soft hand touched my arm.

"Sir?"

"Not a fan of crowds."

"Of course."

I put on my sunglasses, took up my white stick and carry-on bag:
a leather messenger that held my laptop, phone, passport, and other
special devices for the blind I'd brought with me. My lifelines.

"Can I assist you? Or call someone at the gate?"

I wanted to say 'yes' so bad I could taste it. But I had three iron-
clad rules:

1. Never miss a concert
2. No holing up in hotels
3. Don't ask for help unless absolutely necessary

I had to do as much as possible on my own, I reasoned.
Otherwise, what was the point?

"No, thanks. I got it."

I disembarked, and used my cane to find the dimensions of the
tunnel that led from plane to gate. It was quiet in the tunnel. Safe. Then it
ended and the Vienna International Airport opened up before me. Right
away I knew, with that famous Harlan certainty, that I was utterly fucked.

A wall of sound. No, a *cavern* of sound. Sounds pummeling me
from a million different directions and angles, distorting the dimension of
the space and completely obliterating any hope I had of navigation.

I froze. My chest tightened and my palms clutching the cane were sweaty. How in the ever-loving hell did I think this was a good idea? That I could do this? I *couldn't* do this. I wasn't off the plane thirty seconds, and already I was done. It was impossible.

No! I inhaled through my nose, and tried to ignore how I felt almost exactly the same as I had standing on the ledge in La Quebrada, mustering the nerve to dive.

A soft hand on my arm startled me.

"You are on Level 3," said the woman, the stewardess from the plane. "The level is one wide, but straight hallway. Customs is at the end. Beyond that, the elevators. You will need to go down to the first level. There is baggage claim and then you can find the train or…?"

"Taxi," I said, swallowing down my panic.

"Taxi, yes. But please. Let me call an attendant to help you."

"No, no, thanks," I said, feeling better already now that I had at least the smallest of ideas of the layout. "I can do it. Thank you."

"It's no trouble, really."

Irritation flared. My old nemesis. It was laughing at me, showing its teeth. *You think you can beat me? Just wait.*

"I can do it," I said through my own clenched teeth, then forced myself to smile. But Christ, the line in the sand between where I was and where I needed to be for Charlotte was so long and so deep, even *I* could see it from a mile away.

The stewardess let go. "If you insist, sir. Enjoy your stay in Vienna."

I can do it. Just do it. Like the ad says.

I started to walk.

My cane tapped from side to side, unobstructed, but the sheer size of the airport was overwhelming. I felt it open above and all around me, and my skin broke out in gooseflesh and sweat at the same time. I don't know what you called the anxiety that gripped me: the opposite of claustrophobia, but with the same panicky overtones. Overhead speakers made announcements in German, French, and English. Conversations, close and far, were a background hum, though some whizzed past, growing loud and fading, as people walked by. Many people. Too many fucking people. My flight had been a red-eye; it was nine in the morning in Austria. A new day. And it sounded as if the entire country were bustling about the echoing halls of this airport.

I found Customs, but only because I bumped into the guy at the end of one of the lines. And waiting in line, I came to learn, was a contingency I hadn't prepared for. It seems like the easiest thing in the world: you stand in line. The line moves up, you move with it. Except that I had no way of knowing when the line moved. I stood as close as I dared to the guy in front of me; a man who smelled of leather, coffee, and the sterilized airplane cabin. I'm sure I looked like a skulking creep, towering over him, but it worked. When I felt him move, I moved, carefully using my cane at his heels to keep a sense of distance. Finally, it was my turn.

"Passport, sir."

I'd already had it clutched in my hand for fear of holding up the line by fumbling through my carry-on. I went to offer it up and smacked my hand into the bullet-proof partition that separated me from the Customs guy. I felt my neck burn as I found the little space below where you slide your documents.

"Are you visiting Austria for the purposes of business or pleasure?"

"Pleasure," I said, though I knew already that was a big fat lie.

"Anything to declare?" he asked.

"Only my pride."

"Pardon?"

"Sorry, nothing. Nothing to declare."

I heard him stamp my passport and then felt it touch my fingers. "Elevators are to your left. Enjoy your stay."

I moved left—or what I thought was left. My sense of direction was shit. What I thought of as 'left' was often not left enough or too much. I had countless barked shins from my townhouse days to prove it.

I found a wall and a drinking fountain instead of a bank of elevators. I almost bent to take a drink, as if to show I'd meant to be there—and to quench my blazing humiliation. But that would be too pathetic, even for me.

I felt around for my phone, hoping the street navigation might somehow work in here. I could ask it to find the nearest Starbucks—there's always a Starbucks—and then ask a barista where the damn baggage claim was. I could even be bold and buy a coffee while I was at it.

"Directions to Starbucks," I told my phone.

"Starting route to…Starbucks," my phone replied. "Head northwest along concourse three."

Northwest?

"Fuck me," I muttered.

I was wracking my brain for another bright idea that didn't

involve me walking aimlessly, when I learned that Austrians didn't stand by and watch dumb blind guys flail helplessly without doing something about it.

An older man's voice addressed me. "Was brauchen Sie?"

"Uh…The elevators?"

"You are American?"

"American," I agreed.

"What you need? Baggage?"

"Yes, baggage claim. If you could tell me where—?"

"Ja, okay. Kommen."

He took me by the arm, and tugged me.

"Wait, sorry. If you could just tell me where to go…?"

"Eh?"

I could picture the guy blinking at me like I was some kind of moron for resisting his help. And he was right. It was quite obvious that my rule about not asking for help had to die a swift death. Before I even left the airport. It just wasn't possible to do this without help, and it wasn't like *getting* help would make this trip a walk in the park. I mentally modified Rule #3: Ask for help without suffering a kick to my pride every damn time.

Respectfully—I hoped—I angled out of his grasp and took the crook of his arm instead. I smiled in his general direction. "Better like this."

"Okay, gut," he said and I felt him shrug.

We walked about ten paces before the man stopped and said, "Rolltreppe." A nano-second later I learned that was German for *escalator*. I nearly lost my balance trying to find the downward rolling step, and my heart dropped somewhere to the vicinity of my balls as I clutched at the railing.

"Es tut mir Leid. Langsamer," the man said. "Uh, slower? I go slower."

*If you don't fucking mind…*Humiliation burned my neck. Langsamer, I thought. I'd have to remember that one.

We took two escalators down to the main concourse, and then the airport's size swelled to even greater heights and widths. Evidently the baggage claim was roughly six hundred miles away, as we walked for ages in this loud, crowded, cavernous mini-city, where the sounds bounced up and down, all around; each one amplified and multiplied to infinite numbers. The smells of coffee and hot food came and went, and while I'd have killed for a strong coffee, stopping was out of the question. My guide was on a mission, and I was too freaked by the unknowable enormity of the airport to do anything but be led.

Finally, we arrived at the baggage claim; I heard the trundle of suitcases, the whirr of conveyor machines that spat out luggage, and voices. Hundreds of them. The place was packed, and the reality of how unprepared I was hit me again like a lead weight. So many contingencies I hadn't even considered. Like how to know which baggage wheel was mine, or which fucking bag to grab as they went by. The old anger flared, like sneering laughter.

"Die Airline?" the man asked.

"Uh, Austrian," I said. "From New York City."

"Kommen."

My guide tugged me through from one morass of people to another. "Here. I go. Ich bin spät." I felt him pat my arm, his voice was heavy with concern. "Viel Glück, junger Mann."

"Danke," I said. "Vielen Dank."

A grunt of acknowledgement and then he was gone.

Cut off from my anchor, I was adrift in a sea of black sound. A storm battered me; people standing too close, speaking words that meant nothing to me; no way to orient myself, no memory to rely on. This was insanity and I felt less than sane, standing in the hub of all that chaos.

For Charlotte. You're doing this for Charlotte.

The thought calmed me a little. I inhaled deeply several times, concentrating on my breathing, letting the people part around me like a rushing river around a stone. Having no way to identify my bag, my grand plan was to wait until the crowds thinned. After everyone else had grabbed their luggage, I'd see if I could feel what remained, or find an airport worker to help me before they put my bag in the lost luggage jail.

After about ten minutes of standing in the overpopulated blackness, trying my damndest to look casual and not panicked or pathetic, a soft hand touched my arm.

"Are you waiting for your bag?" A woman, and American. She laughed sheepishly. "I mean, of course you are. We all are."

I smiled wanly. "I'm waiting for the crowd to thin out a bit."

"Oh, you don't have to do that! I can help. What does it look like?"

"It's blue and kind of big. The rolling kind."

The young woman went silent for a few moments, then, "Maybe this?"

I heard her struggle and bent to help. Together, we hauled a bag over the side of the conveyor.

"Here's a tag...Noah Lake. Is that you?"

"That's me. Thanks, very much."

"Sure thing," she said and cleared her throat. "Do you have someone coming to pick you up?"

"No, but if you could point me in the direction of a taxi stand, that would be awesome."

"I'd be happy to help," she said brightly, and it didn't escape me that the tone of her voice had changed to one I remembered well from my past life. The light, feathery sound of flirtation. And then I felt her hands on me, as she gently turned me around.

"Straight ahead are automatic doors. Go out and turn right, past a little café, and it's right there."

The vagueness of her directions made my teeth ache, but this woman must have seen my hesitation.

"You know what? Let me take you there myself. We can stop at the café...I'll buy you a coffee?"

In my past life, I would have taken her up on that. And beyond. To my hotel and a mid-morning roll in the sack, maybe. Then a late lunch, more naked gymnastics, and finally a smoothly executed getaway that left no hard feelings or attachments. I marveled at how easy it all had been...and how far away I was from that guy. I only wanted Charlotte, would only *ever* want Charlotte. My love for her ran so deep, it left room for nothing else, not even curiosity.

"That's kind of you to offer, but I have to get going," I said. "Thanks again."

I gave the woman what I hoped wasn't a dickish smile, and followed her instructions toward the cabstand. Or tried to.

Before I left New York, Lucien and I had debated what I would need to bring to survive and not bog me down as I traveled. I brought the barest minimum of clothing to wear for every day, but for Charlotte's shows, I'd had to bring something nice. Lucien tried to talk me out of it, but my overriding need to not look like a fucking schlub won out. I had to bring a suitcase large enough for two suits, and added finding dry cleaners in every city to my quest.

But that fucking luggage. It took me exactly 3.2 seconds to determine it was going to be the bane of my existence. Rolling it behind me with one hand and holding my white stick in the other made me feel like someone had chopped off my left arm. My shield arm. Plus, it was heavy as hell, and I tried not to think about what it was going to be like dragging that thing on trains or buses, from city to city.

I exited the airport, felt the carpet under my feet turn to cement, and headed right. Slowly. Christ, I was slow. Not just slow. *Timid.* The controlled chaos of the airport morphed into an untamed wilderness of a strange city. The sounds of cars alone—so many cars—filled me with dread. I had to remind myself that they were just cars pulling slowly to the curb to let people in, and not death machines driven by crazed maniacs.

I moved forward until my tapping cane struck an obstacle. I hoped it was the cabstand sign, but it was someone's heel.

"Eh?"

"Sorry. Taxi?"

"No, no, dieser Weg. Kommen."

This time, the man took my arm and I let him. *As if you have a choice.* He led me down the sidewalk a few more feet. "Here."

I waited in the cabstand queue for a good twenty minutes until it was my turn. A cabbie—at least I hoped it was a cabbie—took my luggage from me and I felt my way to the backseat of the cab. I slumped into it, feeling as if I'd just played sudden death chess for fifty straight hours.

"Wo gehst du hin?"

"Uh…Grand Hotel Vienna?"

"American?"

"Yeah," I said, leaning back.

"Oh yeah! Go Yankees, eh?"

I offered an unenthusiastic thumbs-up. "Go Yankees."

The Grand Hotel Vienna was an expensive luxury hotel, chosen by Lucien because of its concierge services. He'd booked me in five star hotels in every city, so that I'd never be without first-rate help in English, should I need it.

But this hotel was a few minutes' walk to the Gesellschaft der Musikfreunde where Charlotte would be playing for the next three nights. It was risky to stay so close, but Lucien had insisted on making things as easy as possible in Vienna, my first city, until I got acclimated to the whole experience.

I let the bellboys take my luggage, and lead me to the front desk. I checked in and readied my credit card, but learned Lucien had paid for this hotel himself. A little bon voyage gift. A wave of homesickness crashed over me so strong I had to grip the counter for a second.

I was led again to the elevators, then my room. I tipped the bellboy with a €10.00—identifiable to me by the fold I'd made in its corner. When he was gone, I slumped on the bed, savoring the merciful silence. The stillness. The fact that I didn't have to feel my way anywhere but the bathroom, and that I could do with no curious or pitying eyes on me.

I wanted to sleep but Rule #2 reared its ugly head: No holing up in hotels.

With a groan, I hauled myself off the bed, hauled my luggage *onto* the bed, and started to unpack. I felt my way around the room to get its layout, put the clothes in the dresser, hung up the suits, and then turned to my messenger bag that carried all my lifelines.

Navigation was my first priority. Prior to departure, I actually did go to the Helen Keller Foundation for a cramming session on how to get around. They advised me to bring earbud headphones so I could listen to directions as I walked the streets of the strange cities, and outfitted my phone with a program called Lingo that would translate any phrase or word I asked it to.

They also gave me 3x5 notecards, each marked with a polite request for assistance across busy streets, printed in different languages. The idea being, you stand on a street corner, holding a card into the black ether and wait for someone to investigate. They read it, and help you cross. Sounded all well and good…in theory.

In real life, the idea of standing on a corner like that was one tiny step away from begging. I took the cards with a polite smile and a mental promise to myself to never use them. But somehow they'd ended up in my messenger bag. Lucien, I reckoned.

Second to navigation was not being ripped off or robbed. I had a money reader that was the size of a business card. I slid the bill into the reader and it would tell me the denomination. I'd then fold the corner of the bill a certain way, so I could tell how much it was before I put it in my real wallet, which I kept on a belt that tucked into my pants. My credit cards were in there as well, while I had a dead credit card and fifty Euros stashed in what I called my bait wallet—one I kept in my jacket pocket. If someone tried to rob me, I'd give them that, and hope it would be enough.

I set up my laptop, with my writing software, on the suite's desk that faced a window. I felt the sunlight on my hand, and turned my face to it, allowing myself a moment of satisfaction. I had done it. It sucked and was mentally exhausting in a way I couldn't have imagined, but I'd made it. I was in the same city as Charlotte, and tonight I'd be in the same room with her.

Eating dinner in the hotel restaurant, getting a cab to the concert hall, and making my way to the will-call ticket booth were each and every one fraught with difficulty and stress, but at four minutes to seven, an usher led me to my seat: last row, upper level, closest to the door so I could make a quick escape.

I slumped into the plush chair, my white stick propped between my knees, utterly wiped out. My earlier satisfaction was obliterated. This was too much. Too hard. Too stressful to cast off again and again, into unknown spaces, without the slightest ability to get my bearings. I had made it to the concert hall, but at what cost?

The orchestra, Charlotte among them, tuned up, and then the crowd around me erupted with applause—the conductor taking his place at the podium I guessed. A silence and then…music.

I had no idea of the program, of course. I recognized nothing of the four or five pieces they played, but it didn't matter in the slightest. The music washed over me, and carried me along its soft currents. Charlotte's violin was indistinct from the rest of the orchestra, but I imagined I could hear her anyway. She was there. In the same room with me, even if that room was enormous, and she and I at opposite ends. My Charlotte was there, and I could feel her; her energy and love and everything she poured into her music. I felt the stress of the day loosen its grip on my mind and muscles.

That feeling, that euphoria of possibility, reinforced the idea that I was doing the right thing. It was quite obviously going to be harder than I ever foolishly imagined it to be. The hardest thing I'd ever done, but wasn't that the point?

I wouldn't give up. I couldn't. The long, black road lay stretched out before me, but I would walk it because Charlotte Conroy was waiting for me on the other side.

The Darkest Road

The tour moved and I followed. After Vienna, to Venice, a city of immeasurable beauty and uniqueness, now reduced to a maze of precarious walkways, squares filled with flapping pigeons and pigeon shit, and narrow streets that dead-ended at sandstone walls. Then on to Florence, where the cobbled streets threatened to trip me every other step, and its famed art remained locked away on the other side of the black curtain.

I wish I could say it got easier, but it didn't. Countless missteps and obstacles marked every hour, and I considered a good day one in which I didn't get hopelessly lost. I made it to Charlotte's shows, but the effort it took to do so was extraordinary.

There are too many details to list; a litany of frustrations and embarrassments that left me with teeth clenched, rage boiling beneath the exhaustion, my skin scarlet with humiliation. I held up busy lines trying to pay for tickets or lunch or coffee. I suffered the polite silences, but impatient sighs of clerks and tellers, waiters and hotel concierges, as I fumbled my way through ordering food, or picking up dry cleaning, or lugging my fucking bag onto a train that was already crowded.

I had to ask for help everywhere, every day, of strangers as they passed by, snagging them as they went, and hoping they'd forgive my intrusion. Or—worse—interrupting conversations with terrible German or halting Italian, praying for an English speaker to tell me which seat was mine? Which way to the ticket office? Which way to the cabstand or train station or hotel front desk? *Which way to Charlotte?* I wanted to scream, and fall at her feet and touch her cheek, her hand...just for a moment, to remind me what it was all for.

Crossing streets in the dark, sticking close to other pedestrians, feeling unasked for hands guiding me, or yanking me out of the way of oncoming cars whose horns blared my humiliation for everyone around me to hear. Using those stupid cards the Foundation had given me because they actually worked and I'd have been road kill without them.

The vast majority of people on the planet are kind before they are cruel, but I didn't escape the snickers and jabs of the not-so-kind. I caught stealing hands on trains, and felt the jolt of fear surge through me, wondering what would come next? To be left alone? Or maybe a knife sliding between the ribs by a more insistent thief? I had no way of knowing, of assessing the people around me for potential danger. I had to trust. I had to hope. And sometimes, I just straight-up prayed.

Words that had never, in my past life, been used to describe me hung over me every day. Helpless. Slow. Hesitant. Lost.

And that was just the first week.

I called Lucien at night to check in, and told him again and again, I was fine, the lie rolling so easily off my tongue. I emailed Charlotte once that week, speaking into my little machine that didn't translate the weariness or the longing of my voice. Just words. To her, black lines on a white screen, that didn't reveal one hint of the struggle behind them. I told her I loved her and that I missed her, and that I was working to make myself whole so that we could be together, because it was clear to me that I'd have to shatter first, and be put back together. This journey was going to break me down in every way, and I'd either arise from it victorious, or it would destroy me, and the way things had begun, I worried it would be the latter.

And then it got worse.

Rome
⠠⠗ ⠕ ⠍ ⠑

On the overnight train from Florence to Rome, a migraine woke me from a shallow doze in my sleeping compartment. I slept with my bag of lifelines under the thin pillow, and felt inside it for the little bottle of pills. The train jolted and they all spilled into my hand.

All three of them.

I struggled to remember the last time I'd had a migraine. It had been awhile. Was it the one that nearly killed me? The one that ended with Charlotte saving me, bathing me, and the kiss that had changed everything between us?

I swallowed one Azapram dry, and made a mental note to tell Lucien to send me more. The migraines were pretty infrequent so I'd probably be okay for the rest of the tour, but better safe than sorry. One Monster with no Azapram would do me in.

And I was walking a thin line, already. The old anger and bitterness—the absolute hatred of my situation—had been awakened, and each difficulty was another log on the fire, until the inferno was raging. I felt feverish. My teeth clenched, and I had to remind myself to loosen up before the Monster awoke again.

Rome was a city of art and history, but to me it was just noise and smells and people and an infinite number of ways to become hopelessly lost. What was the Sistine Chapel to me? Or the Pieta? Or even the Coliseum? Another loss to contend with; another battle to fight against bitterness: I was visiting the world's oldest cities, and all that made them magnificent was locked away from me but for vestiges of memory.

I tried to appreciate Rome as I was, not as I wished I could be, for wasn't that one of my goals too? *The* goal? I couldn't stay in my cushy hotel. I had to face the enormous, crowded, chaos of the city, to soak it in as best I could. Experience it as a blind man, and find the soul of Rome—or any other city I visited—without *looking* for it.

On a more practical level, I planned to have lunch, buy a gelato or a cappuccino, and then prepare for Charlotte's show that night. But Christ, the complications embedded in each one of those acts were enough to make me want to tear my hair out.

I walked from my hotel to the Trevi Fountain, obeying the commands of the GPS in my ear. I arrived without incident, without getting lost, or honked at. A minor victory. I felt pretty good. The sun was warm but not stifling, and the sound of the fountain was soothing. I envisioned the droplets catching the sun and sparking like diamonds for a brief moment before disappearing into an impossible blue basin.

I sat for a long time, and may have even smiled. The rage that boiled just beneath the surface was reduced to a simmer for the time being. Charlotte might be sightseeing with her friends. It wasn't wise to stay too long in one place. I decided to use my GPS to find a café and grab a late lunch before heading back.

I stood up quickly, and the sudden pain almost knocked me back down. The Monster had been awakened by my movement. The back of my head glowed white hot almost at once, and I caught my breath.

Again?

I'd just subdued a migraine the night before. Was this the same pain, having escaped from the Azapram, or was this another? I felt in my bag for the pills and took one. Only one remained. I reached for my phone to call Lucien and tell him to send me more. Then the earthquake hit.

It had to have been an earthquake, didn't it? Why was the ground tilting? I stumbled sideways, as if I were a failing Vaudeville performer and the big hook had come to yank me off the stage. I got my elbow up in time and pain radiated all up and down my arm, and then my hip, as I struck the ground. My white stick clattered and rolled. My bag hit hard, and I had a flash of worry for all the devices in it I needed to survive. Immediately, voices and shuffling feet surrounded me; grabbing hands sat me up.

I held my hand out to nothing, as if I could hold on to whatever was making the lazy spin I felt in my body, and slowly it stopped. Voices bombarded me with questions I couldn't answer.

"Stai bene?"

"Posso chiamare qualcuno per voi?"

"Chi è con questo uomo?"

I felt around for my cane and someone pressed it into my hands, while someone else slipped my bag over my shoulder. More strange hands helped haul me to my feet.

"I'm okay," I said, my voice a croak. "Okay, grazie. Grazie mille."

"Where do you go?" asked one man in a thickly accented voice. "I help."

I was about to politely decline, but my legs felt like jelly and my hands shook. The migraine was roaring in the background. *What is wrong with me?*

"Where do you go?" the man asked again. "Hospital?"

"No, no. No hospital. Hassler," I managed. "Hotel Hassler."

I heard whistling and shouts, and then I was being guided into a cab—or so I hoped. My rescuer climbed in beside me.

"Per favore, Hotel Hassler, e rapido."

"You don't have to…" I started, but gave up. I didn't know how much English my helper knew and the cab was already moving anyway.

It had been a short walk from my hotel to the Trevi: the cab arrived in less than five minutes. I dug for my wallet, but felt a hand on my wrist.

"No. Sit."

I nodded weakly. Sitting was good. Lying down would be better. After some back and forth in Italian, the door opened on my side and my rescuer was helping me out. He guided me up the steps and into the cool of the hotel. I knew he'd led me to the right place—the sounds and smells were as I remembered them.

"Va bene, adesso?"

"Uh, sure. Thank you. Thank you, very much. Let me pay you for the cab…"

"No, no." A rough hand patted my shoulder. "Prenditi cura di ti. Take care, eh?"

Another nameless, faceless stranger, here and gone again. My world was populated with them; guardian angels I would never meet again, but who made it possible for me to take the next step to Charlotte.

I made my way to my room on the third floor, and sat on the edge of the bed. I wanted to collapse down and sleep, but something damn close to fear held me rigid.

"It was the heat. And exhaustion," I said.

And the migraine? Two in two days. That's never happened before.

"Stress," I answered, and that seemed right. God knew I was stressed beyond all reckoning, every fucking second of this trip.

Faint relief loosened me and the exhaustion swooped in. I told my phone to text Lucien for more Azapram in the next city—Barcelona, Spain—and then set a timer for a nap. I wanted to sleep for a million years, but Charlotte had a show that night and I couldn't miss it. Rule #1.

I woke in the throes of my usual nightmare, choking on nothing, struggling for air. I sucked in a deep lungful, and tried to remember where I was. A bed. I was dressed—jeans and a t-shirt. My shoes were still on and the room felt hot and airless.

Rome. I'm in Rome.

I pushed the button on my watch. *The time is 6:07p.m.*

Fuck! I thought I set a timer, but apparently I screwed that up too. Charlotte's show was at seven. That gave me less than an hour to shave, shower, dress, eat, and find my way to the concert venue. In my state, I needed *at least* two hours to accomplish all that. And that's when I wasn't feeling as if my bones were filled with lead. But missing one of Charlotte's shows was out of the question.

Pushing all my fears and unease over the dizziness out of my mind, I felt around the side table for the hotel phone. After a few frantic tries, I found the button that called the front desk and ordered a plate of spaghetti, because that was all my feeble brain could cough up. Italian food=spaghetti. Pathetic.

"And your wine?" the woman asked.

Italians didn't get out of bed without a glass of Chianti first, judging by how many times I'd been offered wine in Venice and Florence.

"No wine. Just water. Please."

I felt my way to the bathroom, to the electric razor I'd set up by the sink. I shaved my thin scruff of a beard a little thinner, then wrangled the water temperature into submission in the shower. I was hurrying as fast as I could, but once the water hit me, I slumped and turned my face to the spray, my weariness expanding and spreading through me with the water's heat.

Charlotte. Where are you? Why aren't you here with me?

As if on cue, desire for her rampaged through me, swift and hot. My body missed her as much as I did. Fiercely.

With my sight gone, I experienced intimacy with Charlotte almost entirely through touch. I couldn't look at a photo of her, and soak in her smile or the beauty of her hair falling around her face, or the swell of her breasts against her dress. I had to touch her to remember her, as all of my memories of her were sensation only.

And god, I missed touching her. I missed the way her lips felt on mine as she smiled. I missed the silky strands of her hair through my fingers. I missed the soft weight of her breasts in my hands. I missed her kisses, especially the maddening way she'd skim her tongue over my lips, then graze her teeth with a hot little gust of breath, before finally giving me her whole mouth, granting me entry. Christ, just that kiss made me hard. Every time.

I imagined it then, of having her in the shower, up against the wall, naked and wet; her skin warm and slippery…I groaned and took myself in hand, needing the release, the relief. Some shred of pleasure in this wasteland of misery.

But I couldn't have even that. My supersonic hearing picked up a knock on the outer door. Room service. I didn't have time to finish, and figured it would probably be best to *not* greet the guy with a raging hard-on. I turned the water to icy cold and the heat of passion, imagined though it was, flamed out. My anger, however, only burned brighter.

With a tray of delicious-smelling food waiting for me, I ran my hands over my suits, trying to remember which was the dark gray sharkskin, and which was the light navy. I couldn't concentrate. My fingers, like tired eyes, couldn't focus. I spent a good five minutes I didn't have trying to remember where I'd put my goddamn ties. By the time I was dressed, the spaghetti was cold but I sat down to devour it anyway.

After, I threw on my suit jacket and shoved my lifelines into my messenger bag, but for my phone. I asked it how to say, "Where is the ticket office?" in Italian and then spent another few harried seconds searching for my goddamn white stick that had rolled under the bed.

"*Dove si trova la biglieterria?*"

"Great. How do you say 'fuck me' in Italian?"

"*Fottermi,*" my phone helpfully replied.

"You got that right."

I asked the concierge to hail me a cab for the Teatro dell'Opera di Roma, and slumped heavily in the backseat. My phone said it was ten minutes to seven while the GPS in my ear said the drive was fifteen minutes long.

"Fottermi," I muttered. That one would come in handy, I thought.

Traffic was bad. At least I guessed it was judging by the herky-jerky starts and stops of the cab, and the intermittent swearing and honking I heard up front. I was going to be late, there was no way around it. And if the venue was the kind that didn't allow late-comers to skulk in, I was fucked.

But seriously, who cared? All this goddamn rushing for nothing. For what? To listen to my girlfriend, but not see her? To not even hear her, if I were being honest; she was just one of three or five or however fucking many violinists a symphony needed. The bastards didn't even have the sense to let her play solo, so why the fuck was I bothering? What was all the toil and suffering for? To make myself better? This wasn't *better*!

Rage boiled through my blood, and that old Monster-conjuring hate writhed and coiled through me like a nest of snakes. How did I ever think that this would work? Or that Charlotte would even be there for me when all was said and done? What if she was pissed that I was right there the whole time and she never knew it? Or if she thought it pathetic that I followed her around Europe like a stray dog whose owners had moved on without him? What if she got sick of waiting?

What if she met someone else?

My leg had been bouncing with impatience but stopped dead at the thought. Every part of me ran cold and my rampaging litany went silent.

What if Charlotte had met someone else?

Yes, wondered the snide voice in my head. *What if she met some guy, some musician in the orchestra? A flautist with a big instrument he wanted her to blow?*

"Shut up."

"Che cosa?" my cabbie demanded.

I ignored him. I had more important questions to answer. Such as: with whom was Charlotte spending all her time? Some dorky musician, perhaps, who could talk about librettos and sextets and tempos until the fucking cows came home? Or a suave bastard who took her to sidewalk cafes and bought her gelato or coffee or wine? Enough wine to get her tipsy that he could steal a kiss and she could decide she liked it? That she liked *him,* this guy who could see her face and tell her how beautiful she looked in the Italian moonlight, and who could visit museums with her on their off-days, or the Sistine Chapel, or the Trevi Fountain…

A guy whose advantage over me—besides his perfect 20/20 vision, of course—was his *presence.* He was there for her, sharing her journey, and while it wasn't in Charlotte's DNA to cheat on me, her heart was big and generous and full of love she was eager to share, that she *needed* to share.

Why not? It made sense that she'd fall in love with a musician, a more cultured man who didn't swear as much as I did, or have *vision problems*, or mood swings, or …*who didn't get drunk and allow her to be assaulted in an elevator by someone you called a friend?*

Or that.

My fevered and jealousy-choked imagination even composed a sound bite of the email I was now sure waited for me on my laptop when I got back to the hotel.

Noah, I'm sorry. I didn't mean for this to happen...

My hands clenched my white stick like it was her new boyfriend's throat. I nearly told the cabbie to turn around. Towel thrown. White flag up. Stick a fork in me, I was done.

"Okay, Teatro," the cabbie said, and I realized the cab had stopped.

I didn't move. I didn't want to. It was too fucking much. Too hard.

Quit your whining. You're here, so go listen to her.

Well, why the hell not, I thought with a sneer. I had nothing better to do.

I paid the fare, and made my laborious way to the venue. Ushers guided me to my seat—always last row, corner—and I listened to some damn concerto or sonata or whatever the hell it was, waiting for the music to soothe me as it so often had other nights. Not this night. This night I was as impervious as a brick wall; the musical notes bounced off me like pebbles.

One piece ended, and the audience returned respectable applause while I thought about slouching down and having a nap. With my sunglasses on, who the fuck would know? And did I care anyway? Nope, I surely did not.

And then it happened.

A lone violin began to sing a soft, melancholy melody while the orchestra played behind—gently, as if not to disturb the soloist's simple song. A delicate web of silver hung in the black of my imagination, whorls and garlands of sound, emerging from that single violin, until the entire Teatro was glistening in my mind's eye.

I listened, hardly breathing, and when it ended, the audience was hushed. One heartbeat, one breath, and then an eruption of applause ten times louder than for any piece before.

I turned to the person on my left, found the delicate wrist of a woman. "Who was that?" I asked, and motioned at the stage. I hoped this lady spoke enough English to reply, though my heart already knew the answer.

"The program says her name is Charlotte Conroy," said the woman with a Middle Eastern accent. "I have never heard of her, but she was quite extraordinary, wasn't she?"

"Extraordinary." I sat back in my seat, and the next piece began—some rambunctious Italian rondo I barely heard.

Okay, baby, I answered, because Charlotte had been speaking to me, even if she hadn't known I was there to hear it. She hadn't met someone else—the idea was ludicrous to me now. She was waiting for me, and her heart ached for me as much as mine ached for her. I heard it in her music, as plain as if she were speaking words.

My anger melted away like wax in the hot sun.

I won't give up, I promised her. *I won't. No matter how hard it gets, I swear to you, Charlotte, I'll keep going. For you, baby. For you...*

I climbed out of my chair the moment the last note of the last piece dissipated in the air, and headed back to my hotel, determined to make a fresh start in the morning. No more whining, no more tantrums. Charlotte was still waiting for me and I'd be damned if I didn't do everything in my power to make her heartache mean something.

I lay in bed feeling better than I had in days, and dove into what I hoped would be a deep, restorative sleep...

...that lasted maybe all of an hour. I woke up with pain raging at the back of my head. I barely made it to the toilet before vomiting up my $43 plate of spaghetti, and flailed around—in profound agony—to find my bottle of Azapram. One pill left. I took it with trembling hands, and swallowed it down.

And now I had none.

Barcelona
⠀

The Monster was faster than the mail.

My first night in Barcelona was spent riding out a migraine. I had no pills to take. I'd called the front desk for some aspirin, but that was like putting a band-aid on a gushing artery.

I sat in the bathroom of my five star Barcelona hotel, banging down the seconds until the migraine's iron-tight grip on my head began to loosen. At first, I thought I was merely delirious with the pain, but no, I sensed a gradual lessening from molten agony, to plain agony (a huge step up) to a really fucking bad headache, to finally none at all.

A sound like a sob burst from my chest and throat, and I threw my arm over my eyes, sucking in deep breaths. *I can't do this anymore,* I thought. *Enough. I'm done.* But I couldn't be done.

I hit the button on my phone. *"The time is now 8:10 a.m."*

I thought of all I needed to do today before Charlotte's eight p.m. show. Dry cleaning and laundry, lunch and dinner, finding the concert hall…Too much.

So quit, came a thought.

"No," I told it and the empty room.

That's the third migraine in five days, came another.

"Fuck you. I'm stressed."

But the little sliver of fear that had wedged itself into my gut when I'd lost my balance in Rome, dug deeper. The idea that something was wrong with me was like a weed in my mind that kept trying to take root and no matter how many times I yanked it out, it grew back.

"*No,*" I said again, into the black. I was just tired—more than tired. Exhausted from this ordeal, constantly stressed out and fearful of being robbed, lost, or ruined, and missing Charlotte so badly I could hardly breathe.

Still…

I snarled a curse and hauled myself off the bathroom floor. Dizziness assaulted me at once. The room canted and tilted under me, like a ship tossed at sea. I braced myself on the counter, while my fear poured in and tried to sink me.

It passed. *You sat up too quickly and you haven't eaten. Nothing tragic about that.*

I had to eat. I felt weak as hell, and I couldn't venture out to do

49

the laundry much less anything else, until I'd had some food. I felt for the phone on the nightstand, and my fingers trailed over the buttons hoping for one that felt more prominent than the rest. They all felt the goddamn same. I pushed one at random and heard a recording, in Spanish, of what I presumed was an ad for the hotel itself. One of those informational things that are constantly playing with soft music behind them.

I slammed the phone down and picked it up again. I felt at the numeric keypad, and was relieved to find that 0 was still alone, at the bottom, where it should be. I pushed it, hoping for an operator. I got one. A young woman answered.

"Buenos días, recepción. ¿Cómo puedo ayudarte?"

"Yeah, do you speak English?" I asked roughly.

A pause. "Sí, señor. How may I assist you?"

"I want to order some breakfast. Room service."

"Very good, sir. What will you have?"

"I don't know." I rubbed my forehead and my eyes that felt tired, even though they'd had the last two years off. "Food. Breakfast. I don't care."

"Do you need a menu, sir?"

"I have a menu," I said through gritted teeth. "I can't read it. Can you please just tell me what you have?"

"You…wish for me to read to you the whole menu, sir?"

"Yes…No, just…" I thought I was there, at the breaking point. I sucked down a deep breath. "Eggs. Do you have fucking eggs?"

The woman cleared her throat, obviously trying her damndest to maintain her cool with the American dickhead barking at her over the phone.

"We have eggs, sir."

"Fine. Good. Eggs, coffee, toast…whatever. Just bring it. Room 42."

I slammed the receiver down, and a second later I swept the phone and everything else that was on the side table onto the floor. My hands were shaking. My breath came in harsh gasps. *What is happening to me?*

I took several deep breaths, concentrating only on the in and out until the urge to scream or smash something else faded. I stood on trembling legs and felt my way to the bathroom, where I splashed cold water on my face. I lifted my face to the mirror. On the other side of the black curtain was a haggard man, pale and sickly, with bags under his dark-circled eyes. And the eyes themselves—that Charlotte found so attractive—were haunted and dull. Their useless stare more blank and empty than ever before.

I didn't have to see to know that. If Charlotte saw me now, she'd cry. Ava would yell and *then* cry. My mother would weep and my father curse me for hurting her again. And Lucien…

I stumbled back into the bedroom, stubbing my toe on the lamp I knocked off the table. I found my phone on the bed, buried under the covers. I nearly called Lucien, telling myself it was just to hear his voice. To talk to someone who knew me so I didn't feel so goddamn trapped. But I knew if I called him, it wouldn't be to chit-chat. I'd tell him to book me a flight home that very night.

Do it, said the voice of reason that so often sounded like Ava in my mind. *You're done.* She was right. I couldn't survive another migraine without the medicine. Not now.

"Charlotte, I'm sorry," I croaked and started to push the button on my phone when a knock came at the door.

"Room service, señor."

I held the phone in my hand, my head dropping from exhaustion.

Another knock. The button on my phone was smooth under my thumb.

"Señor?"

I drew in a breath, as if I could suck in strength and fortitude and courage from the air around me. *Charlotte…*

"Come in."

"Your breakfast, sir." I heard a tray set down. "And a package has arrived for you. Just this morning."

I held out my trembling hand. "Show me. Please.

"Of course."

A cool, dry hand took mine and led me to the tray, to a square package wrapped in paper. I tore it open and a bottle fell out, rolled onto the table.

"What does it say?"

"Az…Azapram…"

"Fine, good, thank you. Go. You can go now."

I sat on the bed for a long time while my breakfast grew cold, turning the bottle over and over in my hand. Twelve capsules. That's all they'd give me at a time. But if the migraines kept up at this rate, I'd be out in two weeks.

Quit. Just quit.

But I didn't. Charlotte had never quit on me. Never.

51

I got up and ate my breakfast.

Amsterdam

I persevered through that breakfast, and dozens more after, but the writing was on the wall: I was breaking apart just as I had predicted. The raging anger in Rome had degenerated into desperation in Barcelona, and worsened through Nice, Paris, and Brussels; a terrible erosion that left me feeling hollowed out. I was below anger, somewhere. Under the stairs in a lightless basement. A dusty crawlspace. Or in Sylvia Plath's bell jar, maybe, where everything was airless and stale.

By the time I hit Amsterdam, I was about done in.

It was around nine in the morning when the train from Brussels arrived at the Centraal station, and a hand jostled me from a shallow doze. I dragged my bag off the train, with help from someone—the conductor, maybe—and then dragged myself into the terminal.

"Information desk?" I demanded of someone I felt walk past me.

I called it going fishing: I cast out a line—my arm—hoping to snag someone who could give me the information I needed. It had been humiliating to do it at first. Now, I didn't bother with niceties. Niceties were too tiring.

"Uh, yes," said the guy I'd caught. A young guy, maybe my age. "Okay, this way."

He led me to the info desk, and from there I was guided to the cabstand with a waiting taxi. Cab rides were usually a reprieve. Mustering the willingness to exit the known space and safety of a taxi for the unknown of a street or some hotel rattled my nerves and left me drained. But I was already drained and my nerves seemed to have fallen asleep. I rode in the cab. I paid the fare. I got out, que sera, sera.

In my deluxe fucking luxury suite that I couldn't see or appreciate, I found the king bed and wanted to face-plant straight into it and not move all day. But I discovered I wasn't really tired. Mentally exhausted beyond all reckoning, yes, but mostly I just didn't give a fuck.

I unpacked my bag and went about my process—not because I needed or wanted to, but because I couldn't think of a reason not to. Or anything else to do. Just one mechanical step after another.

I laid out my suit for Charlotte's show the next night; the VTO had the night off which meant I did too. I arranged my devices, set up my laptop, and then wandered the perimeter of the room to get its dimensions and orient the bed to the bathroom.

I took a scalding hot shower, wondering if that would kick-start my body. It didn't. By then, it was noon, and I decided to head out for lunch. I had to. If I laid down in the bed, I wouldn't get up again. Not for days, maybe, and when Lucien called, he'd hear it in my voice that I had to stop.

After eating lunch, I sat at my table at the café and vaguely wondered what I should do with the rest of the day. I had been to Amsterdam in my past life. A beautiful city of canals with bicyclists riding over the stone cobbled streets; important landmarks and history. The Anne Frank House was here, but what would I get out of that? A small and dwindling voice urged me to go and just experience it as I was. That I'd feel the momentous history of that place, even if I couldn't see it, and to miss out would be a terrible waste.

I opted to miss out.

Then there was the Van Gogh museum. Priceless art not three feet from my face, and it may as well be chicken scratch.

It may sound like I was feeling sorry for myself, but in actual truth, these losses had no affect on me. Just facts I had no way of changing, and couldn't be bothered to care about in the first place. Was that progress? Or acceptance of my fate? I told myself it was, but that same little voice whispered it was the furthest thing from it.

I had to get out of this funk. It was so deep, it wasn't even depression. Just nothingness. I asked the waiter to give me the name of another café. A different kind of café, that sold more than food. If I couldn't change my reality, I'd bend it a little and just let go of *thinking* so damn hard.

My waiter gave me a name and helped me hail a cab.

"Café J," I told the cabbie. Nope, no Anne Frank or Van Gogh for me. I was going to get high, and fuck it all, that sounded like the best idea I'd ever had.

It was early afternoon. The streets were all but empty when I got out of the cab. It sounded like the café was tucked into a sleepy little corner of the city. But people—not me, but real people—had jobs and worked and didn't smoke pot at 2:04 in the p.m. on a weekday. Inside the café, I expected some tourists at least, but couldn't tell from the muted conversations if there were any other Americans there.

"A joint, please," I told the guy behind the counter. The place felt dim and cozy, but I imagined neon lights behind the counter or maybe menus of colored chalk.

The guy cleared his throat. "Uh, okay. Can you be more specific?

We got about a hundred different strains."

"Surprise me," I muttered.

"More expensive, better quality," he said. "But you gotta buy a coffee too."

I smirked. "Yeah, that makes sense. A stimulant to go with my depressant."

"Huh?"

"Nothing. Coffee, black. And your most expensive cigarette. Are we on a canal?" I thought I smelled the water, but couldn't be sure, as the café itself was pungent with a variety of other strong aromas.

"Yeah, you want a canal seat? I can help you."

Either Dutch pot baristas were customer service fanatics, or the fact that I paid the equivalent of $33 dollars for one fat joint made him go the extra mile, but the guy walked me through the café, to an outdoor terrace, and sat me down on a couch. I heard a few talking voices around, but the couch I had to myself. For the time being.

"Your coffee's on the table to your right." The guy pressed a book of matches into my hand. "You want me to light it?"

"Nah, man, I'm good. Thanks."

And after two hits on the joint, I *was* good. Better than I'd felt in eons. I'd paid a premium and that's what I got.

"Primo shit," I muttered and laughed at myself.

I hadn't laughed in forever. That felt good too. My whole body felt good, and I could feel—but do nothing about—the stupid, lazy grin on my face.

This was a better apathy. My bones melted into the couch, and the blackness that entrapped me felt lighter somehow. All the heavy thoughts and grief and the pain of missing Charlotte that had been weighing me down were now weightless and drifting. I waved them away and they vanished into thin air. *Like smoke*, I thought with another laugh. I sat back on the couch while my coffee grew cold beside me.

I honestly don't know how long I sat there; time oozed by, marked by conversations around me that came and went. I had presence of mind enough to let my joint go out before it was halfway gone, or else I'd probably have slipped into a coma. Thoughts of food infiltrated the green haze around me, but to get off that couch was much too much effort. Instead, I decided to do something I'd never done before on this entire trip, and that was strike up a conversation.

There was a small group of people who were now sharing my couch on my left. The pot was making me bold. Or stupid. Or boldly stupid. I turned to them and said, "Nice day for it, yeah?"

A pause. A silence. I just laughed, and then they laughed too, and just like that, I had four new friends. All youngish—my age, or close to—and all college students, all able English speakers.

Bram's handshake was rough and strong, like his voice.

Schuyler was the jokester, his handshake loose and light, like his laugh.

James was a Brit; he gave my hand one stiff, formal shake and called me "mate", his voice fully loaded with curiosity.

And Anika was soft and sweet, and smelled like caramel. She shook my hand and held it. I realized she wasn't going to let go until I pulled away.

My new buddies bombarded me with questions: why I was there, who I was with, and what the fuck was a blind guy doing all alone in Amsterdam? I answered all their questions with a moronic lack of caution, and someone helped me light the joint again.

"What do you do for a living, Noah?" James asked.

"I'm…uh, I'm a writer," I said.

That was the first time I'd said that. It felt strangely arrogant. Had I done enough to deserve the title? I thought of all my articles for *Planet X* and gave myself permission to use the word.

"I used to write for a magazine. Now I'm a freelancer…so to speak." I laughed, thinking how I 'wrote' by dictating into a machine. "*So to speak*. Yes, exactly! Get it?"

They didn't, but they all laughed the way high people laughed: just because.

"And why are you traveling around Europe? Are you alone?" Schulyer asked.

"Seems bloody mad to me," James added quickly.

"My girlfriend is a violinist with a symphony," I answered slowly, trying to make the words that came out of my mouth match the words my brain wanted me to speak. "She's on tour and I'm following her…It. The tour. Research," I added. "How a blind person would travel Europe. That's my book."

Yeah, that sounded okay. Sloppy, but enough truth to be believable.

Anika sidled up to me and cooed. "Awww, you're doing it for your girl. For love! You're doing it for love!"

"Yeah," I said, smiling lazily. "That too." *That most of all.*

I shared my joint with them, and while I'd clearly already won

Anika over, that brought the guys around. Instant best buddies.

"Fuck me, mate, this is some strong shit," James said, coughing.

"Neuk mij dood," Bram said and it sounded like he was pounding his chest. "Sterk. That's *strong* to you, Amerikaanse."

"It's primo," I said helpfully.

"Primo!" Schuyler said with a screeching laugh, and we all laughed with him.

"Do you speak Dutch, Noah?" Anika asked excitedly. It seemed like everything she did was excitedly. She couldn't sit still. I could feel her vibrating next to me, like a live wire.

"I speak French," I said.

"Ohh, I love French. So romantic. Tell me, what do you say to your girl in French to get her hot, eh?"

The others laughed. I managed a smile.

"She doesn't speak French."

"No? Too bad. What a waste." Anika leaned closer. "I speak French. Maybe you will say something hot to me, oui?"

Naturally, I hadn't the faintest clue what Anika might look like, but right then I was hit with a very strong impression: a girl with a soft face but hard, cold eyes. Of warm skin but a bruising touch. A slapper. Someone who would hit a man and then cry hysterically after, begging forgiveness.

"Anika, niet een slet van jezelf niet te maken," Schuyler laughed. "Noah, thank me. I just told her not to make a slut of herself in front of you."

"Slet?" Anika shrieked in my ear. "Here's some *English.* Go fuck yourself, Schuyler!"

Schuyler just chuckled and knocked my knee with his hand to get my attention. "Hey, you need to learn Dutch, ya? I teach you. Say this one. Very important: Neuken in de keuken."

"Noykehn in de koykehn," I muttered, feeling stupid. I took a hit off the joint and felt instantly less stupid. "What's that mean?"

"Fuckin' in the kitchen," Schuyler said, and laughed like a hyena.

"Sort of loses something in translation," I said. "If you want something to rhyme…'Fuck in the truck.'"

We all burst out laughing at this, the dumbest conversation in the history of the spoken word.

"Schuyler, idioot. Teach him something he can use," Bram said. "Noah, say, Ik moet mijn zonnebrils avond dragen."

57

"That's not going to happen," I said dryly.

"It means, I wear my sunglasses at night," Bram said. "And you do, ja?"

"Ja," I said, smiling softly as an old memory echoed faintly in my mind. "Like Bono."

"Like Bono!" Schuyler screeched.

Everyone laughed so hard, I knew they had to be high as kites, and the vague disquiet I felt for my new 'friends' was relegated to background buzzing. We talked and laughed at nothing, and made stupid jokes until I could no longer feel the sun on my face.

"Eh, Noah!" Schuyler said, suddenly. "We're off to get dinner and then…you'd say 'clubbing.'"

"Have you ever been to a dance club in Amsterdam?" Anika asked. "You must come with us!"

"Yes!" Bram bellowed. "But which? Paradiso? Escape, or—"

"Escape," I said immediately. "Escape."

"Noah wants Escape," Schuyler cried. "Let's help him escape!"

Anika linked arms with me, and they led me out of the café on a cloud of pot, laughter and maybe even a little bit of danger. I felt it, lurking just beneath the surface, but hadn't the faculties or the energy to investigate. Over the last month, my instincts had become a fifth sense, drawing me away from situations—or dark alleys—I could feel, but not see.

But these four moved too fast, and I was caught up with them like a swimmer tossed by a wave—helpless to do more than tumble along until it let up. And god help me, the part of me that had craved danger, that had sought it like a drug, *enjoyed* this. The lightning that skimmed along my nerves was a million times more potent than the pot.

We scarfed down broodje sandwiches from a sidewalk café, and then the gang took me to Club Escape in Bram's car. I thought it must have been much too early for a nightclub but before the loud, pulsing music swamped me, my watch told me it was close to 8 p.m.

"You have a talking watch?" Anika shouted in my ear. "Super cool!"

My sluggish and sound-drowned brain couldn't come up with a response, but it didn't matter anyway. Anika tried to drag me to the dance floor but I refused. I was high, but not so stoned out of my mind that I was about to dance in front of anyone.

I resisted the tug of her small but strong hands. "I wanna sit. Smoke."

The music was too loud and the place was packed with bodies. Too many people. If there was a fire or some other emergency, I'd be done for.

That's just the pot making you paranoid. You should quit.
Why? Charlotte isn't here. She's safe.
And what about you?

Fuck it all. I was tired of the routine, the regimen that I'd prescribed myself. I was going to go where the night took me and suffer the consequences later. My biggest threat, my stupid, cloudy mind reasoned, was keeping Anika's grabby hands off me without pissing her off.

"Where are you staying, Noah?" James asked.

"In the red light district," Schuyler said. "All American tourists stay there. Get high. Get some girls, ja?"

"No. I'm at the Sir Albert."

A silence and then, "The Sir Albert? Oh la la," Schuyler laughed. "Are you a prince? Noah, here, is American royalty. Prince Noah!"

"No, man. I wish. I'm just there for one night," I said, cursing my loose tongue.

Rule #4: Don't advertise you have money while being blind as a goddamn bat.

"I'm splurging for one night," I said again.

"Sure, sure," Schuyler snickered. "*Just for one night.*"

Inwardly, I cursed myself. I felt them assessing my leather jacket, my watch, my sunglasses—the designer brand Ava bought for me. *Prince Noah?* asked the snide commentator who had taken up residence in my mind. *Yeah, prepare yourself, Highness. You're about to get royally fucked.*

I listened to them chat in Dutch—even James, the Brit, could speak it—and, sure enough, I could feel the air between us change. It grew colder somehow. Eventually, the gang decided it was time to bail, and I was hustled into Bram's car, and wedged between Anika and James.

"I think it's time I called it a night," I said.

"No, my man, we're going to a party at my place," Bram said from the front seat. "Canal views," he added with a dark laugh. "You will love."

"I'm sure," I muttered, trying to think how to get out of this predicament with all my body parts intact. But the pot had slowed me down, and Anika was all over me. She had turned sideways to press her breasts against my shoulder, while her hand ventured up my leg.

I caught her wrist and held it. "I have a girlfriend," I said harshly. "This is not going to happen."

"What is *this*?" Anika whined and then laughed. "*This* is nothing but a little fun, ja? A fuck in the truck!"

"No." I pitched my voice to the front of the car. "Bram. Pull over. I'll get back on my own."

He didn't reply, and Anika had nothing more to say to me, apparently, but she had plenty to say in Dutch. The four of them talked all around me and they weren't laughing anymore.

You're a fucking idiot, I told myself, but of course it was too late.

The car stopped, the engine cut out, and two doors opened: the front passenger, and the left rear. Schulyer and James exited, leaving Bram behind the wheel and Anika beside me.

She straddled me at once, and removed my sunglasses to run her hands through my hair. "Ooh, you're so pretty, Prince Noah," she cooed. Her hips undulated, grinding against me. "You and I, we'll play. Let's speak beautiful French together, and then you pay me, ja? For giving you such a good time."

From the front seat, Bram lit a cigarette. James and Schuyler were outside the car somewhere, standing guard I supposed, wherever the hell we were.

I sighed.

My high had been blown away by the severity of this situation, but these four didn't know that this wasn't my first rodeo. I'd been mugged in Queens after subway surfing, and again in Hell's Kitchen, where Charlotte lost her violin. Moreover, this journey had worn me down to the quick. I was all out of fucks to give.

Anika's hands were on the fly of my jeans, trying to work down the zipper. I grabbed both her wrists hard enough to make her yelp, and tossed her off my lap. I heard her head hit the passenger window as I made a dash for the other door.

"Aiii! Bastaard!"

She kicked at me while I fumbled the door open, keeping a tight grip on my white stick.

"Bram! James! Hij mi pijn!"

I scrambled out of the cab, heard shuffling feet over concrete, and then a fist connected with my right eye socket. It felt like a sledgehammer and ten times stronger, since I couldn't see it coming. But my apathy of earlier was a weapon now. The pain seemed distant.

Meaningless. I brought my white stick up and felt it connect with someone's groin to satisfying effect. Schuyler, judging by the little weasel's pained squeak. Good.

I dodged a blow I felt coming, and moved left, to keep myself from being pinned between my new *friends* and the car. But Bram was on me before I could take a step.

"You touched Anika?" he asked, grabbing me and holding me by my jacket lapels.

"He did," Anika shrieked. "His hands were all over me, and when I said he'd have to pay, he knocked my head!"

I couldn't imagine for whose benefit this little charade was for, but the ridiculousness of it made me laugh. "For Christ's sake. I didn't mean to hurt you—"

"You think it's funny?" Anika's slap struck my cheek—a crashing cymbal of stinging pain that radiated up my face and left it burning.

"Oh, Anika." I chuckled tiredly. "I knew you were a slapper."

I don't remember much after that.

I put up a good fight, I think, but I was outnumbered and out-sighted. I got a few good ones in on James and Schuyler but Bram was a boulder rolling down a hill, and I was crushed underneath.

They took both wallets—thief bait and real—my watch, my damn *sunglasses*, my cane, and—worst of all—my bag that had my phone, my money reader, and my text-to-voice scanner. All my lifelines. Thank God I'd had enough sense to leave my passport and some emergency cash in the hotel.

They left me, curled and bleeding, on a street somewhere. I heard the squeal of tires and then all was quiet. No other cars, near or far. The only sound was the buzz of some overhead street light. I smelled brackish water and my own blood, leaking from my nose, mouth, and chin.

For a long while, I just laid on the pavement, my head reeling, the ground spinning under me. I squeezed my eyes shut, and felt my consciousness fade in and out, like a bad radio signal.

"Just go out," I muttered and I finally did.

St. Marit

"Hey."

A woman's voice. A hand touched my shoulder gently.

"Hey. Ben je oke?"

I woke up fully and pain did too. All over my body. It took a moment to remember what had happened last night, and then the memories—sounds and remembered blows—hissed and prodded at me like a poltergeist.

I sat up slowly. "Where am I?"

"You are in the parking lot of my work," said the woman quietly. She sounded young—about my age—and smelled of shower soap and some earthy-smelling oil. "Were you hit in the head? Your eyes are little unfocused."

"I'm blind," I muttered. "It's not new."

"Oh. I'm sorry."

"So am I." I reached for my watch to find the time but my watch was gone. Everything was gone. I had no money, no phone. Nothing. *Yep. Royally fucked.*

"Can I call someone for you?" the woman asked, and helped me to stand.

"No. Uh…no, thanks." I winced. Every part of my body hurt and yet, irony of ironies, no migraine. Go figure.

"You were robbed, yes?" the woman said. "You need the police. And a doctor."

I waved my hands. "No police. No doctor. I just need to get back to my hotel. Somehow…Where am I again?"

"Outside A-9 Graphika? In Amsterdam Noord."

From what I remembered, Amsterdam Noord was across the river from the city center, and somewhat more industrial. Not as tourist-friendly. I gingerly touched a hand to my swollen lip. *Ha. You can say that again.*

"You don't happen to see a cane lying around, do you? Or a bag…?"

"No. There is nothing like that."

I nodded, realizing none of this mattered. Nothing mattered. My lifelines were lost. I was utterly done. I didn't even bother sending Charlotte a mental apology.

"On second thought, would you mind calling me a cab?" I asked. "I have money at my hotel…"

"No. I have a car. I'll drive you." She shifted beside me. "My name is Marit, by the way."

"Sorry, yeah, I'm Noah," I said dully. "Thanks for the lift, but don't you have to work?"

"Not yet. It's not even 6 a.m. I always go in very early. I have time."

"Yeah, me too," I muttered.

My journey was over. I had nothing but time.

Marit had a tiny car that I had to fold myself in half just to sit in, and she drove like a maniac. Or at least it felt like it to my aching face. We drove in silence, though I could practically feel the curiosity radiating off her.

Finally she said, "You know, when I asked your name, I had the silly hope you'd say it was Matt Murdock."

"Who?"

She laughed sheepishly. "Matt Murdock is the name of Daredevil. From the comic book?"

"Never heard of it."

"Oh, it's an awesome story. He's blind, like you, but he fights crime in New York City."

"How does he fight crime if he's blind?"

"The radioactive chemicals that took his sight gave him super-enhanced senses."

"Lucky him."

"So, when I saw you sitting there in the parking lot, blind and all beat up, like after a tangle with the baddies, my imagination immediately went to Daredevil." She coughed. "Silly, I know. I just really love comic books. I'm a geek, as you Americans would say."

"Is that what you do at your work? Draw comics?" I didn't particularly care, but talking to Marit took my mind off the night before and all the nights ahead.

"Oh, no. I'm a graphic artist, but not for comics. I wish!"

I made a sound that would've passed for decent conversation amongst grunting pigs.

"You want to talk about what happened?" she asked after a minute.

"Not really."

"Okay," Marit said gently. "You don't have to talk."

"Thank you." I leaned my head against the cool of the window. Amsterdam sped by on the other side of the glass, and on the other side of my impenetrable dark. Goddamn, but I was sick of it, and it was obvious that I'd never stop being sick of it. What was that John Milton quote Harlan once recited to me? That being blind wasn't miserable, it was being unable to cope with blindness that was misery.

Yep. Milton knew his shit.

A screech, and then the car came to a halt.

"We're here," Marit said. "I'll park and walk you to your room."

"You don't have to."

"You don't have your cane. And your face...Um..."

I touched my bloodied nose. "It's that bad, eh?"

"It's not good."

Marit led me to my suite, where I immediately went for the bed, and lay back. My ribs ached, as did my stomach, as if I'd done a thousand crunches. I heard Marit rummage in the bathroom.

"You don't have to stay," I said.

"I know," she called, "but I can't leave, either. My mother tells me I'm the neatest of her children. My teachers too, in school. I always cleaned up the messes. And you are a mess."

She pulled up a chair next to the bed. "This might sting." I winced as she dabbed the cuts and bruises on my face. "Anything broken? Your nose is not. A miracle, that. How are your ribs?"

"They fucking hurt."

"Take a deep breath."

"Hurts more."

"But no sudden, sharp pain?"

"No."

"Good." She dabbed a cut over my right eye. "Ha! I feel like Claire. She's the nurse who patches Daredevil up after he gets in a brawl."

"So this guy loses a lot of fights, eh?" I snorted. "Some hero."

"He usually wins," Marit said. "He just takes a beating first. It makes the victory all the sweeter." I heard the chair she was sitting in creak, as if she sat back. "So tell me, Noah," she said in an overly cheery tone. "What brings you to Amsterdam?"

64

I barked a laugh, then groaned at my aching ribs. I gave in, and told Marit an abridged version of why I was here.

"You know that's crazy, right?" she said quietly.

"*Was*," I corrected. "Was crazy. It's over now. My lifelines are gone. I can't navigate my way to the next city, let alone make it to Charlotte's show tonight. I'm done."

"Okay." Marit's hand touched my arm. "Who can we call?"

"Lucien Caron," I said. "He'll be worried. But I don't have his number. It was in my phone."

Marit asked me a dozen questions to help track down Lucien, and then sat at the desk and made a dozen phone calls.

"Lucien Caron?" she said finally. "Hello. I am calling for Noah Lake? Yes. A moment."

I made my way to the desk and Marit sat me down in the chair that was still warm from her presence. She pressed the receiver into my hand. The anguish in Lucien's voice was hard to listen to.

"Noah? Are you all right? You didn't check in last night. I called your phone. I heard only obscenities and laughter, then nothing."

"Sounds like you spoke to my good buddy, Schuyler," I said and held my head in my hands, hunched over the desk.

"I was on the phone with the airline just this moment to come find you. What happened?"

I told him, sparing him as much detail of last night's events as I could.

"I'm so sorry, Noah. I shall book a flight for you this night. And a car to take you to the airport."

I don't know if it was Lucien's voice, or hearing that it was over from another person, but the numbness I'd been feeling for the last few days started to fall away, piece by piece, and my heart ached as if I'd been struck with a mallet. I pressed my lips together, the goddamn tears welling in my eyes at sudden, terrible pain.

"Noah? Are you still there, my boy?"

"I failed, Lucien," I breathed. "I can't keep my promise to Charlotte. Not because of fate or bad luck, but because I keep screwing up." My chest felt so tight, I had to gasp for a breath, to speak while keeping the dam from breaking. "I failed," I said again, hoarsely. "I failed Charlotte...I failed *us.*"

"You did better than anyone could have hoped, my boy. The journey itself was too difficult. The fact you made it this far is a miracle. You should be proud."

"Proud? I felt nothing, Lucien," I whispered. "I didn't care what happened to me. I was down so deep…just numb. But now…" I sucked a tremulous breath. "Now that I've fucked it all up, I care again. I care a lot. I don't want to quit."

"Don't," Marit said from beside me. "It's none of my business, I know but…I can help. Let me help."

I raised my head, hopes and possibilities struggling to come to back to life. Then I shook my head. "No, you've done enough. I can't ask—"

"You're not asking, I'm offering."

I started to protest but the overwhelming desire to not fail Charlotte was stronger than my despair. Was it possible I could continue? I'd already been to the brink of failure so many times, it felt like I lived there. I thought of the rest of the tour: Copenhagen, Warsaw and Prague, then Germany and finally Austria…Christ, could I make it through Poland or the Czech Republic where the language barrier would be even wider? On paper, it didn't seem like much of an obstacle, but without my sight, every disadvantage weighed a thousand times heavier. And I was already so goddamn tired…

"Let me help. I'll take care of everything." Marit rested her hand on my arm and said gently, "If I were Charlotte, I wouldn't want you to miss it."

"God, I still hope that's true." I mentally braced myself for next few weeks, and heaved a steadying breath. "Yeah. Okay. Thank you."

I told Lucien to wire me money from my savings so Marit could get me a new phone, and to figure out how to send me new credit cards. He sounded dubious at first, but his desire for me to succeed was just as strong as mine. "I shall do my best."

"Aren't you going to tell me to be more careful?" I asked dryly. "You should. Clearly I need to hear it again."

"I am not in the habit of blaming the victims for the crimes perpetrated against them…" I could hear him smile slyly, "though I would ask that you choose your friends a little more wisely."

I listened to Marit bustle around behind me, laying my suit on the bed. "That, I can do."

I got off the phone with Lucien, and swiveled in my chair. "You're not going to get in trouble for missing work?"

"I can take the day. I never miss work. Ever. I go in early, stay late." Her voice quieted. "It's nice to go out for a change."

"Good," I said. "Then let me take you to dinner too. As a thank you."

"You're up for going out to dinner?"

"Rule #2: No holing up in hotels."

"Okay, well…yes. Dinner would be nice," she said, and I tracked her moving around the room to gather her purse and keys. "You need a shower—rather urgently—and then a nap. And I have errands to run. I'll just…okay. Be back soon."

The door shut and I was suddenly alone with my almost-failure. I had been at the edge—again—and been hauled back from the fall.

"For the last fucking time," I muttered as I stepped into the shower. The hot water seemed to wash last night off me, and I felt good. Better. Almost like myself.

How is that possible? You don't know what 'yourself' is.

That was true. The accident had forever altered me. Smashed me up and rearranged all my parts so that I couldn't sort them out. I was blind. That was the only truth I had, and it had become my identity more than my own name.

And that was a fucking terrible way to live.

I stood in the shower until the hot water ran cool. Cool like the rainwater I'd felt on Charlotte's skin the night in New York City, when I'd disappeared on her and she'd searched for me in a storm.

"You deserve more than what's left of me."

"There's so much."

Even then, Charlotte had seen what I couldn't. And right then, under the falling water that felt like rain, I allowed myself to think that maybe she was right.

Marit found an agency with services for the blind. She procured a new white stick and a pair of sunglasses, while I napped. I was putting on my suit when she returned, and heard her suck in a small breath.

"That is a very nice suit, Noah," she said.

"Thank you, Marit," I replied. "I'm sure you look very nice too."

She made a noncommittal sound. "So, this is weird," she said, after a moment.

"What is?"

"Well…It's not every day that girls like me meet men like you."

"Blind bastards, lying in parking lots, bleeding all over themselves? Yeah, we're a rare breed."

She laughed, but it faded quickly. "Noah, before we go out in public together, I think you should know that I'm not really the type for dinners and concerts. I mean, while I was out, I went home and dressed up. And by 'dressed up' I mean I put on black pants instead of jeans and a shirt that doesn't have a comic book character on it. I'm about eighteen kilos overweight, I have dreadlocks and piercings. Tattoos all up my arms—"

I stopped and looked toward her. "What does that have to do with anything?"

"Just…fair warning."

"Well, thanks for the *warning*," I said lightly, "but I don't even know what a kilo is."

"I just mean, we look about as mismatched as can be, you and I, and I think it's only fair that you know that. I know this is not a date," she added seriously. "I'm not putting that pressure on you. You love Charlotte and I'm not going to sit around wondering why you didn't call me tomorrow. But you are…very handsome, Noah. And kind. And it's not every day that a girl like me meets a man who is both, and spends the day with him. It's a little…strange. I'm afraid I'm going to embarrass myself."

"First of all, Marit, you didn't *meet* me," I said, my neck craned to tie my tie. "You found me left for dead in a parking lot. If one of us is going to be embarrassed in this little scenario, it sure as hell isn't going to be you."

She scoffed a laugh. "Well, since you put it that way..."

"Secondly, you saved my ass this morning. You saved my entire trip. I don't know how to repay you but to buy you dinner and take you to listen to Charlotte. And even that is more of a favor to me. I've been to sixteen concerts in the last month, alone. It'd be nice to share her talent with someone…to have someone appreciate her a little, like I do."

"That sounds lovely," Marit said, and I could hear her smile.

"So…we're good?"

"We're good," she agreed, and I knew that was the truth.

"Is it straight?" I asked, indicating my tie.

"No." She approached and her fingers tugged and straightened. The earthy smell of whatever oil or perfume she wore was strong but not unpleasant. "There. Come on, Noah Lake. Let's go before we're late to your date with Charlotte."

I reached out and she put the crook of her arm to my fingers. And yeah, there was more of her to hold but so fucking what? Marit was an angel of mercy and it didn't matter what she looked like. She was beautiful in my mind, and could have been as gorgeous as Valentina in real life, but neither of those facts got her any closer to my heart.

Charlotte owned that particular piece of me. Hell, she owned all of me, heart and soul, but thanks to Marit, instead of heading to the airport in defeat, I was back on that long dark road to where Charlotte was waiting. Saint Marit, that's what she was, and always would be.

We arrived at the Koninklijk Theater Carré, and took our seats in the corner, uppermost row.

"My nose is bleeding," Marit joked. "This is where you always sit? So far away?"

I smirked. "I didn't buy the seats for the view. And I can't let Charlotte see me."

"Well, I'm going to get a pair of those fancy glasses so I can see *her*. The violin players are all bunched together. What does she look like?"

"Do you have a program?"

"Yes."

"If she's doing a solo tonight, you'll see her," I said, and wished I could borrow Marit's eyes just for the night.

"She's playing the andante to Mozart's Sonata in A for piano and violin." Marit shifted toward me. "Is that a good one?"

I smiled. "You'll see."

The concert began and we didn't speak again until Charlotte took the stage. Then Marit grabbed my arm. "Oh, Noah," she whispered. "She is so very beautiful. I can see from here. She glows."

I nodded and clenched my jaw, thankful I had new sunglasses to conceal my eyes. But when Charlotte began to play, I couldn't hold it back. How close had I come to ruining this? Her music was so achingly beautiful, her talent so rich and vibrant. I felt Marit clutching my arm, sniffling now and then, and the ice in me that had begun to crack back at the hotel shattered completely.

I grabbed for Marit's hand and squeezed, my other hand holding my head as I bent over, wracked by sobs I tried my best to keep quiet.

I broke open, broke apart, and let all the rage and pain and bitterness go. It was too hard to hold on to, and I couldn't do it any more. I thought I was holding on to my old life, but there wasn't anything left of it. Only ugly residue, and that, I finally realized, wasn't worth holding on to.

Everything I thought I knew about what it meant to be a man was stripped away. What remained was what it meant to be a man who loved a woman as much as I did. To be a human being experiencing this life in all its ugliness, its beauty, its pain and hate; good and evil; love and death.

So yeah, I sobbed like a goddamn baby, but I'd never felt more like myself—whatever that was, or whatever it was going to be—than at that moment.

After, Marit took me back to the hotel. I tried to get her phone number or email to keep in touch, but she refused.

"You're like a UFO sighting," she said. "You crash-landed in my parking lot and we had an adventure, but now you have to go back." She laughed shyly. "I could tell people what happened but no one would believe me."

I gripped my new white stick and felt the reassuring weigh of my new phone in my pocket. "Thank you, Marit. I can't thank you enough."

"So…remember when I told you it was crazy, what you were doing?"

"Change your mind?"

"No," she laughed. "But it's kind of heroic, Noah. I don't think you see it that way, but maybe you should."

I smiled. "I think you read too many comic books."

"Probably," she said, and I could hear her voice retreating down the hall. "But I love them because in the end, the hero always gets the girl."

Metamorphosis
⠿⠿ ⠿⠿⠿⠿⠿⠿⠿⠿⠿⠿

Through the next few cities, I noticed the change. Copenhagen, Warsaw, Prague…None of it was easy. Not one minute. But the frustrations didn't weigh me down until they buried me. I got pissed now and then, but the anger didn't consume me. I let the experiences in and I took the best of them with me, discarding the rest and starting over fresh with each new day. I talked to people now. I chatted, laughed; had lunches and coffee.

In Prague, a young Swiss couple on their honeymoon walked with me across the Charles Bridge, describing the city's beauty in both French and English, with the hopes I would see it even more clearly in two languages.

In Warsaw, a little old lady helped *me* cross the street, and then took me to her flat for borscht and bread. I spoke not a word of Polish and she not a word of English, but she gabbled at me the whole time. When it came time for me to leave, she kissed me goodbye on both cheeks, and I felt my chest tighten. Apparently, I'd become a huge sap, and I was glad Ava wasn't there to see me blink my eyes dry or I'd never have heard the end of it.

In Berlin, I asked the concierge at my hotel for a quiet place I could stroll away from crowds, and he rattled off a list of famous landmarks.

"Wait, say that last one again," I said.

"Charlottenburg Palace?"

I grinned like an idiot. "Yes, there. I'll give that one a try."

The tour was weeks away from ending but I felt peace swell in my heart, washing away all the bitterness and anger. But I didn't think to meet Charlotte until the end, in Vienna. I had to make sure this peace wasn't transitory, that I wouldn't wake up one morning and feel as angry as I had in Rome, or panicked as in Barcelona, or the horrific nothing of Amsterdam.

I never did.

The only black spot was the migraines. They came with more frequency than usual, but I managed them. I managed everything instead of fighting it, and while it was still incredibly difficult and stressful, I knew I was going to make it.

And then I woke one morning to feel the sunrise streaming through my Munich hotel room. I felt the gold and orange of the sun on my skin. A new day. The tour moved on to Salzburg on this day and then to Vienna to conclude the tour. But I couldn't wait anymore. I didn't need to. The time had come. Tonight, in Salzburg, I would attend Charlotte's show and then after...

I closed my eyes and smiled while the sun warmed my face, rising high and dispelling the night for good.

Salzburg
⠠⠎⠁⠇⠵⠃⠥⠗⠛

After the short train ride from Munich that morning, I made my way to my Salzburg hotel, shaved, took a shower, dressed. I ordered room service and at ate it leisurely, sipping the best coffee I'd ever tasted. I brushed my teeth, gathered my things, and headed out.

The GPS on the new phone Marit found for me in Amsterdam told me where I could buy a new suit. I was sick of the two I'd been wearing all summer. I wanted something new and sharp for Charlotte. Light gray with a vest, because I knew she liked vests on me. I let the saleswoman choose the tie. Plum purple, she said, and I thought Charlotte would like that too.

I had the suit sent to the hotel, and then continued strolling. Lunch was at a cozy little bistro, also a short walk away. The Salzburg's downtown district was very small. The worry that I might bump into Charlotte flared up but then I remembered that was perfectly okay. If I didn't find her today, then tonight.

I'm going to be with Charlotte tonight.

Before I headed over to her concert, I bought her flowers at a nearby boutique. A dozen red roses. The clerk put them in my hand and my not-unpleasant anxiety ratcheted up a notch. Every minute that passed brought me closer to her. The thought made my heart clang madly; anticipation shivered over my skin. In a fit of extreme wishful thinking— or maybe cautious foresight—I tucked a small handful of condoms into my jacket pocket at the last minute.

Hey, you never know.

Lucien called me while I was in the cab on the way to the concert venue.

"Noah, the most astounding news," he said excitedly. "I wandered onto the Vienna Touring Orchestra's webpage. Their show tonight features Mozart's Violin Concerto No. 5. Our girl is going to be the soloist."

A laugh gusted out of me; a bubble of happiness, bursting. "Should I tell her you said hello? I'm going to be with her tonight, Lucien. It's done."

"Oh, my dear boy. I'm so happy for you. And for her. And proud of you both."

I cleared my throat, and tried to sound cavalier. "Yeah, well here's hoping she doesn't hate my guts."

"It is not possible for Charlotte to hate. She hasn't the capacity."

That was true. My Charlotte was too full of love. But did she have any left for me? Or had the time apart altered her so that she wasn't the same—that we weren't the same together?

Had she waited for me?

At the Mozarteum Concert Hall, my seat was still in the back row, corner. I gave the usher a ten Euro note, the bouquet of roses, and instructions to give it to the soloist after the show.

I clenched the armrests of the chair until my knuckles ached. The program began and Charlotte took the stage; the crowd offered her polite applause. They didn't know her, or what she was capable of. Until she began to play.

I listened to her sing with the violin I'd sold my Camaro to buy for her. Had I once thought that a sacrifice? Damn, but I'd give it again. I'd give more. Everything. Every breath. Every beat of my heart was for her.

And she gave everything to us, her enraptured audience. I could feel it—the sense of awe around me that said we were experiencing the beginning of something extraordinary.

When it ended, I got up from my seat with the vague idea to make my way down to her, but when I rose, the audience rose too. A thunderous ovation filled the hall and my heart clenched so hard, I laid my hand over it.

Soak it in, baby. This is all for you.

I had to let her have the moment. If she were angry or upset with me, my sudden appearance would only ruin it. I made my way up and out, to get some air and regroup. I would go back in once the crowds had gone, and find her.

I made my way outside. The night air was cool but not cold, and I was grateful for the breeze over my skin that felt like it was burning. I found a wall and leaned against it, and then I heard the voice I'd been dying to hear for the last six weeks.

"Noah!"

She was there. Right there. I could reach out my hand and touch her…

"Hey, babe."

She gasped, and my heart stopped, waiting.

"I'm going to fly at you," she cried.

"God, yes," I breathed.

Her body collided with mine and I caught her up in my arms and lifted her off the ground, holding her so tightly, breathing her in. Oh Christ, my Charlotte. I had imagined this moment a thousand times but nothing could prepare me for what it felt like to hold her, or to listen to the gentle, aching cries of her as she held me.

She was just as beautiful as I'd remembered. Beautiful in my arms and under my hands, and in the fierce beating of her heart pressed to mine.

I loosened my hold on her enough to let her feet touch the ground and then kissed her eyes, her nose, her tear-streaked cheeks, inhaling her and tasting her, until our mouths met in a kiss that seeped into every part of me. I kissed her with everything that I had, thinking the pain of our separation and the hardship of my journey here would rush up to swamp me, but I felt nothing but sheer joy.

And love. Above all, love.

"God, baby," I said brokenly against her cheek.

"I know," she cried softly. "I know, I know..."

We remained there a long time. I held her, and she held me, until the concert audience let out, and parted around us, and we finally let the real world back in. And with it, the close proximity of our bodies awoke another need in us.

She took us to a hotel a block away. It felt small, smelled old. Historic. Much too historic for our purposes.

"You'll have to pay," Charlotte said at the front desk. "I have nothing. I jumped off the stage to find you before you disappeared again."

"*You jumped off the stage?*" I didn't wait for an answer, but tossed my credit card onto the desk, and swept Charlotte into my arms again to kiss her hard, my tongue sweeping every corner of her mouth, wanting to taste all of her *right now.* I missed her to the depths of my soul, but my body had missed her too. Badly.

Up one flight of creaky stairs, a key in a door, and then all I knew was Charlotte. Her skin, her hair, her body pressed to me, the scent of her....all of it, *mine.*

Her hands around my neck pulled me down to kiss her, and the second our mouths met, I literally stumbled at the lust and longing that swept through me. I groaned and kissed Charlotte so hard I feared I'd cut her with my teeth, but she was just as rough. I felt the want in her even before her hands tore at my belt.

"Wait, wait," I breathed. "When I tell you where I've been, what I've been doing, you might not like it," I said, slipping the words out between kisses. My god, she smelled so good, tasted so good. "You may be angry. You may hate me."

"Did you murder someone?" she asked, pushing my jacket off my shoulders.

"No," I breathed and kissed her again, groaning because, Jesus, her hands felt like they were everywhere.

She tore at my vest; buttons popped and clattered to the floor. "Did you cheat on me?"

She was being playful, but the mere thought of it punched me in the gut like a fist. "Fuck no."

"Then I'll take my chances."

She pulled me close again, and I could feel her smile on my lips before we kissed again, ravishing each other's mouths.

"Do you want to go slow?" I asked. My thoughts were breaking apart into nonsense under the onslaught of her touch, but I had to make sure this felt right and good for her. "Charlotte…I love you. I love you but I want you. Hard. Tell me this is okay."

"I want you too. I've *needed* you…so badly," she breathed. "It's okay. It's more than okay." She jerked to a sudden stop with a little cry. "But oh…god, we have nothing…"

"Left jacket pocket," I said.

"You're kidding," she laughed, breathlessly, *relieved.*

"What can I say? I'm a fucking boy scout."

She left me to dig out a condom from my jacket and then we took up right where we'd left off—a flurry of hard, aching kisses and touches against the wall of that little hotel.

Christ, I still couldn't believe this was real. After so long, not just apart, but suffering for want of her. She strained to meet my mouth with hers so she could kiss me the way only Charlotte could kiss me. I felt her hot little gust of breath first, so sweet, and then her open mouth brushed mine, her tongue flicking and then retreating. I grabbed her hips and thrust her close to me, craning down for more, but she moved back, just out of reach, and then I felt her teeth capture my lower lip. She sucked it, ran the tip of her tongue along it, then let go.

That kiss. I lost my damned mind with that kiss.

I wanted to tear the dress off of her, but she had nothing else to wear. I hauled it up over her hips instead, and wrapped an arm around her waist underneath. She was wearing a thong; I could feel the bare flesh under my hand and groaned. I felt for the delicate piece of material at her hip and tore it apart.

"*Yes*," Charlotte breathed against my neck, rolling the condom down. "Please, Noah..."

I lifted her legs and she wrapped them around my hips. "Tightly, baby."

Her legs squeezed, holding on, holding her up, drawing me to her. Her nails dug into my skin at the back of my neck. Her mouth was as hot and soft and wet as her body as I slid inside her.

My girl. My love. My Charlotte.

We rocked against each other so that I thought the little old hotel might come crashing down around our ears, but even more than the ecstasy of lust, the love I had for her spurred me. It drove me deep inside her, to make her mine—not as a possession, but as a completion of me.

My life. She is my life.

"Noah," she breathed, then screamed, clinging to me as if she'd never let me go.

Never do. Never let me go...

Thoughts scattered, leaving nothing but sensation. In my dark world, there was softness, heat, broken cries and gasps, and her skin, her hands, her mouth, and the sweet tightness of her body, and the pleasure and love that bound us together, all of it rising to a crescendo and then melting into something gentle and deep.

We satiated that first raging hunger to be together again, and I lowered her feet to the floor. Our biting touches dissolved into sweet, deep kisses; a mellowing of the passion into something long and slow and languid. I kissed her so thoroughly and so tenderly, I forgot to breathe. I had my Charlotte back, and at that moment, I needed nothing else in the world. Not one damn thing.

My hand sought her cheek and brushed away the stray locks of her hair that had fallen loose from some up-do. I felt chagrined now, at the roughness of what we'd done. I disposed of the condom, buckled my pants loosely and smoothed her dress down. She deserved to be cherished slowly but I felt her smile against my hand.

"You were...unbelievable tonight," I whispered, and smiled. "At the concert I mean. Astounding."

"I can't believe you heard it. I can't believe you're here," Charlotte said. Her hands slipped down to my chest, and to the buttons on my shirt, unbuttoning them one by one. She pushed the shirt from my shoulders and lifted the undershirt off to press her forehead to my bare chest. Her lips brushed my skin, over my heart, in a soft kiss.

"I'm so in love with you," she sighed. "And I missed you."

"I missed you. God, did I ever. And I'm so sorry. But I had to—"

She silenced me with another kiss, her mouth soft and wet on mine. "Not yet. Tell me everything, but not yet."

My hands slipped down her back, to the zipper on her dress among the velvety folds. I slid it down and laid my mouth to the smooth skin of her shoulder while pulling the strap aside. The dress, loose now, fell away easily. I kissed her mouth, her chin, and bent to kiss her neck while my hands slid up and down the naked skin of her back. Her hair smelled of vanilla and lilac. Her breath, mint, and her own sweetness. Her tears tasted of salt, and I kissed them, licked them off my lips before kissing her again.

I stepped out of my pants, kicked off my shoes and socks, and wrapped her in my arms. She was so light; I lifted her off the ground so that she was taller than me, her forearms resting on my shoulders, her fingers raking through my hair.

"I like it up here," she whispered. "Gorgeous view."

"Bed?"

"Three steps back."

My legs found the bedspread, and I turned and gently laid her down. We kissed and touched wordlessly for a long time and it scared me how much this meant to me. How much I loved her. But I was triumphant. I slayed the dragons that stood between us, and now was free to love her this much, knowing I'll be goddamned if I ever hurt her again.

"Did you find what you were looking for?" she murmured.

"Yeah, baby. I got myself back."

She stifled a little cry and I gathered her to me, wrapped myself around her and her around me. Her breasts pressed against my chest, our legs entwined. Another condom was procured, and then we were joined in one easy movement. I buried my face against her neck as the sensation of her enveloping me made me shudder.

"How can it feel this good?" I breathed, my face lost in the silky curtain of her hair.

"Oh, Noah," Charlotte said, her mouth at the hollow of my throat. "My Noah…"

Yes. I was hers and no one else's, until the day I die. And with that certainty came the greatest peace I'd ever known.

Interlude

⠔⠀⠒⠀⠒⠀⠶⠒⠀⠆⠀⠒⠒

The following morning I woke to Charlotte nuzzling my neck and laying feathery little kisses along my jaw. She felt so warm and soft, and very, very naked.

"Please tell me I'm not dreaming," I murmured.

"I know what you mean." Charlotte snuggled closer. "I feel like I'm being rewarded for something, but I don't know what I could have done to deserve this happiness."

"Are you happy, baby? Truly?"

"More than I thought possible."

"You waited for me," I said, my hands roaming over her shoulders, her neck, her exquisite breasts; looking at her the only way I could.

"Of course I waited for you. Did you think I wouldn't?"

"This trip wasn't the easiest thing in the world," I said lightly. "I had a lot to worry about."

She shifted and I could feel her studying me. "Did something happen to you, Noah? Tell me. Last night you said it was hard, but that doesn't seem like enough."

"No, but it's enough for now. Right now, I just want to be with you, Charlotte. I'll tell you about it someday, but not *this* day. Okay?"

I felt her reluctance but she nodded, and kissed me, and the kiss started to become more, when a knock came at the door. We were too tangled up together for either of us to want to move, and I sure as hell didn't want to let her go. But the knock came again, accompanied by a voice.

"Zimmerservice? Room service?"

"You?" Charlotte asked.

I shrugged. "Wasn't me."

She extracted herself from my arms and the warmth of the bed.

"Our tawdry affair has left me with nothing to wear," she said. "I'm borrowing your dress shirt, if you don't mind."

She was being playful again but I couldn't muster anything witty to say. I envisioned her wearing only my shirt and nothing underneath, and sucked in a breath. Even more than that, her very presence was still extraordinary to me after what felt like eons of solitude.

I heard the door open, and a hotel clerk rolled in a cart—I could

80

hear the soft squeak of its wheels. A cloud of delicious smells wafted in with it.

"We didn't order this," Charlotte was saying. "Um, wir nicht...um, *order*—I don't know that word—die Frühstück."

"Yes, madam. From our British guests in the room adjacent. There is a note, there," said the clerk in perfect English, and then departed.

"A note..." Charlotte said, and then loosed a peal of laughter. "Oh my god, listen to this." She plunked down beside me on the bed. *"Judging by the sounds from last night, you both could probably use some refueling. Enjoy! Your tired—but amused—neighbors next door. PS, Tonight, perhaps a movie and a cuddle?"*

I fell back on the pillows, laughing long and hard and from the gut, until my sides ached.

"It's not funny!" Charlotte cried, trying to be serious and failing miserably. "Oh my god, I'm mortified!"

"You should be," I said. "It's all your fault; you're so loud."

She swatted me on the arm with the note. "It's all *your* fault I'm loud!"

I grabbed her and flung her, squealing with laughter, on the bed beside me, and covered her body with mine.

"I hope our British neighbors are out for a morning stroll right now," Charlotte said with a sigh as I laid kisses down her neck.

"I hope they aren't." I nipped at the soft skin beneath her ear.

"No?" she breathed, arching into my touch.

I grinned. "Free lunch."

Sometime later that morning, we finally put our clothes back on, and Charlotte made a call to Sabina Gessler, the director of the Vienna Touring Orchestra.

"I don't have to be back until later this evening," Charlotte told me. "I want you to come with me and meet everyone before the concert. Sabina, and Herr Steckler, and—oh! Annalie! My best friend here. She is lovely. I told her all about you. Except that you're blind. Funny, that never even occurred to me. I just don't think of you that way first."

"Neither do I," I said. "Not anymore."

Charlotte gasped. "Really? Oh, Noah..." I heard the bed creak as she stood on it and wrapped her arms around my neck. I breathed in the perfume of her skin. "That's the best thing I've ever heard."

God, this woman. I pressed a kiss between her breasts, over her heart. That sound, her heart quickening its pulse under my touch...the best thing I'd ever heard.

"We have one problem," Charlotte said, slipping her arms down around my waist. "It's nine a.m. and I'm wearing a fancy black velvet dress. The Walk of Shame imagery I have going on here is pretty epic."

"Hey, I'm in the same boat. How many buttons did you rip off my vest?"

"Maybe one or two."

I arched a brow in her general direction.

"Or all of them." She giggled. "So what do we do?"

"Let's go back to my hotel..." I cocked my head. "Unless this *is* my hotel. Is this my hotel? Where are we?"

Charlotte laughed again, a rich sound, and cupped my cheek. "Oh, Noah. You sound so...happy. But tired. You look tired, honey."

I held her hand. "I'm fine, baby. Really. Never better, now that I'm with you."

"You promise you'll tell me what happened? I mean, all of it. Your whole trip?"

I kissed her hands. "I promise. Right now, I need a shower. Or, more specifically, I need to get *you* in a shower. In my hotel room."

"You're insatiable," she laughed. "That doesn't solve my current clothing predicament. You tore my underwear to shreds, mister."

"In my defense, a thong isn't really underwear. It's more of a torture device to drive men insane. And it worked."

"I love how it worked," she purred, her lips brushing mine. "You have something for me to wear at your hotel?"

"Leave it to me. I'll take care of you, baby."

"Mmm." She rested her head against my chest. "I like the sound of that."

Downstairs, we stood in line in a busy hotel lobby, executing a midmorning checkout in evening formalwear, though honestly, I couldn't give a shit what anyone thought of us. Another casualty of my lone trek across Europe was that narcissistic paranoia that everyone was staring at me, and judging or snickering or pitying me. It was dead and gone. Charlotte was chagrined, but I wore the evidence of our nocturnal activities like a badge of honor. I'd been with my woman all night, driving her to pleasure again and again—loudly—and the *last* thing I felt about it was shame or regret.

Charlotte returned the key card, and the clerk tapped at his computer for a minute. I heard a printer churn softly.

"Here." Charlotte pressed a pen to my fingers, and guided my hand so I could sign the credit card receipt on the right spot.

This is how I'll sign our marriage license, I thought. *Her hand over mine, showing me where to sign.*

The thought slipped into the dark recesses of my mind and lit up like a flare. It drove my desire for her into a stratospheric level, when I thought I couldn't possibly love her more.

We took a cab to my hotel that wasn't any newer than the one we'd spent the night in, but larger and more opulent. I heard the difference in Charlotte's oohing and ahhing.

"You travel in style," she laughed, wrapping her arms around my neck. "Is the shower as nice as the rest of this room?"

My hand was already on the zipper of her dress. "Let's find out."

After an interlude under hot water with slippery soap, and then me on my knees before her, on a personal quest to see how loud I could make Charlotte's echoing cries, we finally emerged from the cloud of steam. I dressed in jeans and a long-sleeved shirt while Charlotte curled herself in my bed, wearing only the sheet.

"Are you sure you can do this?" she asked. "I mean, I *know* you can, but…"

"I got it," I said, slipping on my sunglasses. "One dress, coming right up."

"*And* underwear, don't forget."

"Sure, sure," I said, and turned away to take up my white stick.

"Don't you need to ask me my size?" she asked coyly.

I snorted. "As if I don't know your every dimension."

"Damn, but you are sexy."

"Stay right there," I told her, shouldering my bag. "I want to imagine you just as you are: naked and waiting for me."

"Such a caveman," she teased, but when I went to kiss her goodbye, she ran her tongue along the seams of my lips before plunging her tongue inside. "Hurry back," she breathed.

As if I needed the encouragement.

The concierge gave me the address of a boutique in walking distance from the hotel. I spoke it into my phone, put in one earbud, and then followed the directions. The sun was out but a cool breeze took the edge off. I found the boutique easily: women's clothing stores have a distinct perfume, and this store smelled expensive.

I smiled. *Good.*

"Kann ich Dir helfen?" said a saleswoman. "Or…American? Can I help you?"

"Yes, thank you," I said. "Do you sell ladies' dresses?"

It amazed me how easy it was to ask, and the only embarrassment was how it all could have been so much easier had I only let go sooner. But I think we learn things—life-altering things—in our own time, through our own experiences, and nothing else. The rehab place *told* me I could do this. Europe proved it to me.

The saleswoman led me to several dresses and described their shape and color, all with a simple, professional courtesy.

One felt silky and rich; the material slipped through my fingers like melted butter.

"And this one? I want it be beautiful for her, but not too fancy."

"This one is perfect then, for a stroll through Salzburg or a nice dinner, perhaps," the woman said.

"Yes, both. Exactly."

"A tasteful floral patter in pale violet and yellow, draping to the ankle."

"I'll take it."

"But…shall I tell you the price, sir?"

I smiled and shrugged. "If you have to."

I returned to the hotel room, and smiled like a madman as Charlotte gasped over the dress.

"It's beautiful," she cried. "Oh, Noah, but it's too much! So much silk…" A pause. "Wait. Where's the underwear?"

I held up my hands, the poster-boy for innocence and virtue. "I looked all over but didn't see any."

She burst out laughing. "You. Are. Terrible."

I wrapped an arm around her waist and hauled her close. "You'll have nothing on underneath that dress, but no one will know it but me."

"Damn you, Noah Lake," Charlotte said, drawing me down to the bed. "We are *never* going to get out of this hotel room."

But we did. Eventually. We ordered room service, and ate and talked and laughed, and kissed until the kissing led to other activities, and a *second* round in the shower.

Finally, we kept our hands to ourselves long enough to put some clothes on. I had my jeans and a black henley. Charlotte put on her new dress, and I slid my hands over her contours to see how it looked.

"You're stunning," I told her.

"Speak for yourself," she purred. "You shouldn't be allowed to wear any color but black. Ever."

By the time we finally stepped out onto the street, it was near four o'clock in the afternoon.

"I have to be back by six," Charlotte told me as we strolled the streets of Salzburg's small downtown. "Let's eat dinner, then I'll take you over to meet everyone before the concert. Oh! Do you have a ticket for tonight's show?"

"Of course. Haven't missed a single one."

"I don't even know how you did that," she marveled and cleared her throat shyly. "But the reason I ask is that Sabina told me that tonight's show sold out first thing this morning. Word of my solo last night kind of…spread."

I stopped walking. "Are you serious?"

"Yeah," she murmured. "And a local—and very picky—music critic was in the audience last night. He stopped Sabina last night to tell her that…um, he was going to write a review for today's paper, and that he liked me. Quite a bit."

"*Liked* you," I laughed, my heart bursting with pride. "You mean he was fucking mesmerized by you, right? We all were. The entire audience was enthralled. I felt it."

She pressed her face to my shoulder. "Well, maybe. But he probably won't use your colorful language in his article."

"He just fucking might," I said, taking Charlotte by the shoulders. "This is it, baby. Your career is going to skyrocket after this tour."

"We'll see," she said, but I could hear the excitement burning behind her words. And why not? She was a genius and it was about time the world knew it.

We ate at a little bistro where Charlotte ordered her favorite Austrian dish for me: a chicken breast that had been baked with a thick coin of pepperoni on top, its juices soaking into the chicken.

"Holy shit, this is amazing," I said.

"What's amazing is watching you eat and drink, and buy clothes and maneuver your way through a crowded city with such ease." Tears choked Charlotte's words. "I'm so proud of you, Noah. And so happy to see you like this…you have no idea."

I reached across our small table and she put her hand in mine. I didn't know what to say, except I love you, and those words were rapidly beginning to sound insufficient. *Marry you. I'm going to marry you, baby…*

Out on the street, we strolled leisurely toward the Vienna Touring Orchestra's hotel where Charlotte had been staying.

"Every shop has Mozartkugeln," Charlotte told me, describing the little city as we walked. "And up ahead is the Geburtshaus. That's where he was born."

"What about another dress shop? Have you something to wear tonight?"

"I do in my hotel room," she said, and gave my arm a squeeze. "And *underwear*. It's all good and sexy to walk around *au naturale* for you right now, but I'm not going commando for tonight's performance. Uh uh, no way."

"Are you nervous?" I asked, because I sure as shit was. A

pleasant buzz in my chest that she'd have a packed house waiting for *her*.

"Not really," she said. "Except now I know you'll be there. But that makes it better, not worse. And you were always there, weren't you?"

"Yeah, baby. Always."

We stopped and I bent to kiss her. The wind carried a promise of winter in it that evening and I'd forgotten to put my sunglasses on after dinner. I felt a gust sweep of chill wind sting my eyes. My *open* eyes. I pulled away.

"Charlotte, am I kissing you with my eyes open?"

She made a perplexed sound. "Uh, I guess?"

"Do I do that a lot? Kiss you with my eyes open? Or when we...when we're in bed together? And when we're making love? When I lose myself...am I just staring at you? Or...?"

"Sometimes. It's not a big deal."

"Oh Christ, why didn't you tell me? Why *don't* you tell me?"

"I have *my* eyes closed. I don't always notice, you know."

"Well, check will you? God, isn't that creepy? I can't fucking tell if my own eyes are open or closed."

"So what? That's who you are. I would never tell you something like that. Ever."

"I'm going to start wearing my sunglasses, twenty-four/seven." I pulled them out of my jacket pocket and started to put them on.

Charlotte stopped me. "You are not. I love your eyes. I love looking at them, admiring them. I count the little gold flecks in them. Eight in your left eye. Six in your right."

"Very mathematical," I said, my ire melting under her touch, her words.

"I'm in love with your eyes. I'm in love with all of you, including your blindness, so I don't care if you kiss me with your eyes open or closed so long as you kiss me."

Oh damn, this woman. I kissed her and forgot to care about what my damn eyes were doing.

Charlotte broke away with little laugh. "God, Noah. I love you. Just...all of you. I love that you're still a grouch and that you swear like a sailor...I love everything about you. And it's not like anything I've ever felt. But it doesn't scare me. I feel so safe."

"You are safe, baby," I said, pressing a kiss into her hair. "What I feel for you...it's not going to go away. Ever. It's in my bones. It's in my damn *molecules*."

She snuggled closer. "I missed you so much some nights, I could hardly eat or sleep. My heart ached. But I get it now, Noah. I really and truly do. And I'm so happy for you. And for me, and for us."

Certainty and peace. She felt it now, and I smiled.

"Me too, baby," I murmured against the soft silk of her hair. "Me too."

Paris

⠏⠀⠁⠗⠊⠎

Charlotte's career blasted off after Salzburg. The music critic who'd heard her that first night wasn't just the small-town columnist she'd made him out to be. He was Viktor Peltzer, a renowned former conductor, violinist, Mozart historian, and notoriously impossible crank. His review of Charlotte's Concerto No. 5 was no less than a miracle, according to Sabina Gessler, who read it to me the first night I met her.

Conroy's vibrato is resonant. Her musicality, vital and aggressive. Every note and nuance lands with tremendous impact. Her accenting, bowing, slurring, and swells are highly individualized; as if she were making these two hundred-year old, oft-played notes her own. Mozart himself likely never expected the violin soloist to play like Conroy, but I believe he would have been as enchanted by her as I was. It gives me great pleasure and—if I may—no small amount of pride, to be the first to experience this soloist and sing her praises, for I am quite certain that there will be a very loud, very vociferous chorus in the near future.

And there was. A chorus, not only of ecstatic reviewers, but a glut of invitations. The world's biggest and most prestigious symphonies called on her to solo for them, and Sony Music wanted to record her, ASAP. She was immediately too big for the Vienna Touring Orchestra, and Sabina Gessler, being the professional that she was, let Charlotte go with class, and a recommendation for a reputable agent which Charlotte suddenly desperately needed. She would leave the VTO after a final, triumphant performance in Vienna, with happy tears and standing ovations that I know resounded louder for me than they did for her. Her focus was to be as true to the music as her heart and soul would allow. Mine was the pure joy that came with knowing her talent was no longer jailed by grief, but singing for the entire world to hear.

"The Philharmonie de Paris has a spot in their season next week and they've invited me to solo," Charlotte told me in our Vienna hotel room on our last day. "You up for another trip? Or maybe you want to go back to New York...?"

Paris had hardly registered on my own solo journey. The city should have been easier for me, given that I spoke the language, but I'd lost it in the quagmire of apathy and depression. And Charlotte was excited about Paris. She'd fallen in love with the city on her tour, and

89

beginning the next phase of her career there seemed like serendipity.

"Of course I'm up for it. Let's go to Paris."

"Are you sure?" I could feel her study me. "You still look so tired, Noah. If you need a break, we should take one."

"I don't need a break," I assured her. *I need you to be happy.* And I sure as shit didn't go through the hell of the last six weeks learning to function blind just so I could turn around and put the brakes on her career. Fuck that. Sleep when you're dead, as the saying went. There'd be plenty of time to rest after Paris.

Her kiss was sweet and electric; full of optimism, and I had no regrets. But that night, after making love with her and falling languidly into sleep, I had another migraine---my fifth in two weeks, judging by the number of pills I had left in the bottle. It woke me with a jolt, glowing molten at the back of my skull. I sat in the bathroom holding my head, waiting for the Azapram to kick in while Charlotte slept, oblivious.

Fear—like a burrowing parasite—gnawed my insides. This wasn't normal. I had to face that fact. But the next morning, I received a phone call from Yuri Koslov. I'd been sending my old *PX* editor chunks of my memoir as I traveled, and he'd taken on the role of my literary agent with gusto.

"Noah, bratishka. I have news. I sent your pages to a publisher friend I know in New York City. Len Gordon of Underhill Press. Ever hear?"

"Doesn't ring a bell."

"He runs a boutique agency. Very *ooh la la*, if you know what I mean. Big names, he has. And he liked your work."

"Really?" I let this info settle over me, not sure what to make of it.

"Ja, *really*, Mr. Cool," Yuri laughed. "But you need to finish. Have you finished?"

"Not yet. I still need the ending."

"Tick-tock, bratishka. I'll give you a deadline because Len Gordon won't want to wait. He's a friend to me, yes, but he's also big. Big, *big*! So don't fuck up it."

I told Charlotte about Len's interest in my book and she pulled up my laptop. "He's big, eh?" she said, typing. "Let's see if Yuri's exaggerating or...Oh. My. God."

"What?"

"Underhill Press?" Charlotte's hand clamped on my arm. "That's Rafael Mendón's publisher."

I sat back on the bed. "Oh. So...big?"

"Big!" Charlotte threw her arms around my neck. "Noah! Len Gordon read your work and wants to meet with you!" She jounced up and down on the bed with my neck in a chokehold. I laughed and felt warmed by her enthusiasm, but couldn't muster much myself.

"It's not done," I said. "It's in bits and pieces. I'm still writing it every night as we speak. It doesn't even have a title."

"And I haven't read one word," Charlotte said dryly. "When do I get a shot, eh?"

"I don't want you to read it until it's done, baby."

I don't want you to worry about migraines, and breakdowns, and dizzy spells...

But Charlotte didn't need to read my book. She read *me.*

"Did something happen to you, Noah? While following my tour?" Her hands were soft on my chest, her voice gentle. "I know it wasn't easy for you. It couldn't have been. But you can tell me. Did something *bad* happen?"

"I ran into some trouble in Amsterdam," I said, and told her about my four new buddies and St. Marit who saved my ass. I told Charlotte about Amsterdam so I didn't have to tell her about anything else. She sighed when I was done and held me close.

"I thought it might be something like that. Are you all right? Do you want to talk to someone about it?"

"No, babe, I'm fine. I just didn't want to worry you...or upset you over the whole thing. It was stupid of me to be so careless."

"You can't blame yourself when a bunch of criminals behaves like a bunch of criminals." She kissed me hard. "I'm so thankful for Marit. And that you're with me now, and safe."

That night, we flew to Paris and we were busy exploring the city, and meeting with the director of the Paris Philharmonic, and arranging the details of Charlotte's performance. It was easy for me to divert her from reading my memoir. And I was still writing it. Every night. I sat down at the desk in our hotel room and spoke, each word leading me to the end of the book. Asking Charlotte to marry me was that end. I could feel it. A culmination of everything we'd been through, and the exact right ending to the memoir. The only ending I could see.

Paris was the most romantic city in the world. I would do it here; I just had to come up with a proposal worthy of Charlotte. Something to make her swoon and melt; to make her feel cherished and adored. Something big and extravagant and special. A grand gesture. But my weary brain couldn't concoct anything remotely close to that. I didn't even have a ring.

I needed help on this one. Reinforcements. And I knew just who to call.

Charlotte's Philharmonie performance was spectacular in every way, so much so that they asked her for an encore two days later. The Paris musical world threw a conniption over her, and we found ourselves caught up in a whirlwind of interviews and meetings that would have overwhelmed her had Oliver Sanner—the agent Sabina recommended—not shown up to save the day. He organized Charlotte's schedule and set her up with a ten-city tour in far-flung places, from Singapore to Sao Paulo through the end of October, and a recording session with Sony in Los Angeles after the holidays.

"That sounds awfully busy," Charlotte said as we had lunch in a café on the Left Bank. "Ten cities?"

Oliver—who sounded blond and sharp and thin to me, like a No. 2 pencil—laughed lightly.

"This is the season, Charlotte," he said in a thickly accented voice. "You know that. We must strike while the iron is hot, as you Americans might say. You shall be quite famous by the time it is over, of that I am certain."

Charlotte's hand holding mine squeezed. "It's just that we've been on tour all summer. Noah especially…"

"No, no," I said. "He's right. You have to do it, Charlotte." Moreover, I heard in her voice that she *wanted* to do it. She was a fireball of energy and this sort of traveling had been a dream of hers since she was a child.

"Give us a second, Oliver." Charlotte waited until her agent left to make some calls, and turned to me. "I want to be with you more than I want to be *famous*," she said, as if the word tasted bad. "I don't care if that breaks every kind of feminist rule in the book, I'm not going to be apart from you right now. We *just* got back together. Call me selfish or crazy, but if you want to go back to the States, then I'm going with you."

"Charlotte, I don't want to go back to the States. I want to be right there as you turn the fucking world on its head with your talent.

Wouldn't miss it."

I could practically hear her biting her lip. "What about your book? Don't you need a chance to really sit down and finish it?"

"I've been writing it as I go," I said. "That's how it's been, and that's how it'll be to the end."

I kissed her worry away, and she told a very happy Oliver Sanner that the tour was a go.

After lunch, as we strolled along the Seine under the shadows of Notre Dame, Charlotte squeezed my hand on her arm. "I'm so happy for you, Noah. And for me. My dreams are coming true faster than I'd ever thought possible. Only it's a million times better than I ever imagined because I have you to share them with."

"Thank you, baby," I said. "I'm happy for you too. I'm happy that the world is going to hear you. You deserve to be heard."

"So do you, Noah," she said seriously. "I know Len Gordon is going to sign you, and even if he doesn't, you've found another life after the magazine. That's amazing to me." She laughed and nudged me with her elbow. "Now if I could just get to *read* your book…"

My book. It still felt strange how fast I'd arrived at this. I remembered the picnic Charlotte took me on, where we read from Rafael Mendón's latest release and Charlotte told me I should write my own. And how impossible it seemed. Her belief in me, even then, had been so solid and unwavering. Even the picnic itself only happened because she insisted upon drawing me out of the house…

And just like that, I knew how I'd ask Charlotte to marry me.

A picnic. In Paris. Under the Eiffel Tower. Cliché? Maybe. But the picnic is what I thought would make it special. A hearkening back to Charlotte's effort to draw me out of the stifling dark and into the lighted world. To show her how far we've come and how important she was to me. That I lived outside the four walls of that townhouse because of her.

I was lost in the daydream of it when I felt Charlotte's warm hand on my cheek.

"My god, Noah, that smile. What on earth are you thinking about that could make you look so beautiful?"

You, baby. What else, but you?

The One Ring
⠠⠹⠑ ⠠⠕⠝⠑ ⠠⠗⠊⠝⠛

My reinforcements arrived the next day. I went to the airport to meet Ava's plane, alone.

"What...? Where is...How are you here?" my twin sister asked over the noisy crowds. "Where is Charlotte?"

"Rehearsal," I said. "How was your flight?"

"How was my...? How did you do that?"

I laughed. "I spent the entire summer *doing that*, remember? Now do I get a hug, or what?" She moved into my arms, and I held her tight. "I've missed you, Aves."

She pulled out of my embrace to hold me at arms' length. "You too, Noah. I guess your crazy-ass plan worked after all. I knew you could do it."

"Yes, you did. And that meant a lot to me."

"Yeah, yeah, so let's get out of this mess. We have a lot to talk about. First, how are you? You look beat. How are the migraines?"

"The migraines are awesome. Best ever, really."

She socked my arm. "I'm serious."

"They're fine. Under control."

And too fucking frequent. I'd had one just the night before. The Azapram went to work before it got too bad, but the fact another had come at all was starting to scare me. I was grateful my sunglasses hid my eyes. I don't know how much or if any thoughts I had showed up in them anymore, but I didn't want to take my chances. Ava would know I was lying, but I wasn't about to scare *her*.

We began to walk, me on Ava's arm, out of the airport, and I eased a sigh that she was leading me. Yeah, I'd made it to the airport and found Arrivals, but it wasn't exactly a walk in the park. It would always be difficult. The fact that it didn't piss me off or send me into a panic was the victory.

"Okay, so tell me about the fun stuff. Are you really going to pop the question to Charlotte?"

"Yeah," I said, smiling like an idiot. "I sure am."

We took a cab to the hotel, and on the way I told Ava about my picnic proposal, and what it meant given our history. The edge of cynicism that colored all of Ava's words, softened.

"That sounds lovely, Noah. Really. So what's my job? Grocery shopping? Please tell me I didn't fly all the way from London—"

"*All* the way? It's hardly an hour-long flight—"

"—just so I could do your grocery shopping."

"You can shop, yes, but not for the food. Tomorrow, I need you to go out with Charlotte in the morning —shop or brunch or whatever— while I get the picnic stuff. When she's at afternoon rehearsal, help me pick out the ring."

I heard Ava's breath catch, and then she cleared her throat. "Yeah, that...I can do that."

I smiled at her, for even though I couldn't see her, I knew my sister; I could feel how touched she was even though she had a hard time expressing it.

I slung my arm around her shoulders. "You're my second pair of eyes, Aves. Except for Charlotte, no one knows me better than you. I know you'll help me find the perfect ring for her." I grinned. "Or at the very least, keep me from being tricked into spending a small fortune on cubic zirconia."

She laughed, and I felt her get back on solid ground, shields up. I hoped that someday she'd find a man who loved her as much as I loved Charlotte, someone she could be herself with, and with whom she could be happy.

"I love you, Ava," I said. "I'm glad you're here."

"Me too, little bro," she said, and I know she was replying to both.

Charlotte was thrilled to see Ava and I was thrilled that they seemed so close. Ava told a smooth white lie about flying in to surprise us before we left Paris. We ate dinner out, and the next morning, she and Charlotte went out to do "girl stuff," while I went out to local markets and bakeries for the picnic supplies.

Self-doubt is the destroyer of joy. I second-guessed my plan within an inch of its life as I shopped. I bought rich cheese, bread, fruit, sparkling water, and little chocolate truffles at a local market, and the basket seemed so light in my hand. This proposal wasn't a grand gesture. It was just...lunch.

"Help me, Aves," I begged after Charlotte had gone to rehearsal and my sister and I set out on our own. "I need a knockout ring so my little picnic idea doesn't seem so goddamn plain."

"What? You were so excited about it yesterday. What changed?"

"It doesn't seem like enough. What I feel for Charlotte…I feel like I need fucking fireworks or a laser show. Or fireworks *and* a laser show. And one of those planes that drag messages on a banner across the sky…"

Ava laughed. "Oh my god, you are panicking. Relax. Charlotte doesn't need or want any of that."

"How do you know?"

"How do you *not* know?" Ava tucked her hand over mine on her arm. "Charlotte is crazy in love with you. She doesn't want fanfare, trust me."

"She's romantic. I want to do something big for her. Something she'll remember forever. A grand gesture…"

"Noah, you walked across Europe blind for her. I think that qualifies."

I made a noncommittal sound.

"Listen," Ava continued. "Charlotte is a romantic, yes. So what she wants is something *meaningful*. Not big. She'll be swept off her feet if you just…tell her what's burning in your heart for her. You don't need to paint it in the sky."

"I know," I said. "I know you're right. But after all she's done for me…"

"And what about what *you* have done for her?" Ava stopped walking. "Hey. Your picnic idea is perfect, because it's perfect for both of you. You're asking her to marry you, to spend the rest of *your* life with her. Make it something you'll remember forever too."

I grinned. "Why, Aves. I never took *you* for a romantic."

"I'm not," she said, laughing, as we resumed walking. "I just like telling people what to do."

Ava and I walked along the Place de Pont Neuf, to a jewelry shop that sold both modern and antiques pieces.

"Do you have any idea what Charlotte would like?" Ava asked as she perused the jewelry under the glass for me.

"Something small. Light. Light enough that it won't get in her way as she plays, but not some dinky shit, either."

"No dinky shit. Got it," Ava said. "Old or new?"

I thought of Charlotte's two-hundred-year-old Cuypers violin, of the music she made with it, and her endearing love of master composers long dead.

"Old. Something with history in it."

"Atta boy."

We perused the glass-bound displays—or, Ava did. She was just as fluent as I was in French, and she and a saleswoman described to me various rings. It quickly became apparent to me how futile it was; I couldn't get a grasp of the rings' styles, and the ones the sales clerk dropped into my hands felt wrong, somehow.

"Try a mental visualization," Ava said, noting my frustration. "Close your eyes."

"That's not necessary," I said with a smirk.

"Ha! I almost forgot," she said, and I don't think she realized what a huge compliment that was. "Envision Charlotte's hand, palm up. Do you see it?"

I nodded.

"Now imagine she turns her hand over, and what ring is there on her finger?"

"Round. Small, but brilliant. More than one diamond, but not heavy or clunky."

Ava told the clerk what I'd said and she pulled several options, none of them feeling right to me or to Ava.

"Wait, Noah," Ava said after the tenth ring was rejected. She clutched my arm. "That one."

"Ah, yes. This one is quite lovely," said the clerk. "Designed in 1909, it is 14K gold with a cluster of quarter-carat diamonds surrounding a half-carat center, like a flower. Eight diamonds in all, quite brilliant."

She put the ring in my hand and I felt its contours and shape. It was light, but it seemed I could feel its age in my hand. In my mind, the diamonds were starbursts against the old gold. I imagined it on Charlotte's finger—I imagined *putting* it on her finger, sliding it over her soft skin and asking her to be my wife.

"This one," I said, and had to clear my damn throat. "This is the one."

That night, I lay in bed in boxers and a t-shirt, mentally preparing my proposal. I had the ring. Just the fact that it existed in my universe—a step toward my future with Charlotte—made me ridiculously happy.

Charlotte breezed around the hotel room, while she unpacked the bags from her shopping trip with Ava earlier that morning.

"I love your sister so much. She is one of the best people, ever," Charlotte said. "So tough and sharp, but super sweet too, just under the surface. And I'm so happy you got to spend the day with her. What did you do?"

"Nothing much. Hung out."

"Oh yeah? Well, we did girl stuff. Which means mostly shopping. I bought a new dress for tomorrow night's show. Want to see it?"

"Sure."

I rose from the bed and waited while she slipped it on, and then she stood before me so I could look. I began my investigation, my hands lingering longest on her breasts under the silk.

"Getting all that?" she giggled.

"Just being thorough," I said with a grin. My hands roamed all over and then I found the zipper on the back. "It's nice," I said, tugging it down. "But naked is better."

She laughed lightly and danced out of my touch. "Wait, I have one more thing to show you. Go. Sit. There's a chair behind you. I'll just be a minute."

I heaved a breath to cool my blood that was already stirring, and waited with herculean patience for her to change so she could show me whatever cute outfit she felt she needed me to see.

She emerged from the bathroom. "I'm ready."

Her voice sounded different; breathy and tremulous. I sat up in the antique French chair that was probably older than Napoleon Bonaparte, and listened as she approached. Her perfume came first—something light, like lilacs over her own vanilla scent. Then her hands were on my knees, gliding up and down my thighs.

She leaned over me, brushed her lips over mine softly, then kissed me.

"Would you like to see what I'm wearing?"

I nodded, stricken mute. The blood had rushed out of my brain, due south, even before my hands found the lacy thong around her hips, or the garters and stockings over the smooth skin of her thighs. My breath caught as my hands went up, finding the silk of her naked back, and then a little nothing of a bra; her breasts were spilling out as she leaned over me.

"Color?" I managed.

"Pale pink," she breathed, and carefully, gently, rested her knee on my aching groin, and rubbed. "Do you like it?"

"Yes," I growled, my hands all over those gorgeous breasts.

"Can you see it?"

I nodded, putting one lace-clad nipple in my mouth and sucking.

"Good," she managed, her words coming out on breathy little exhales of want. "Because I want you to see me, wearing this for you, Noah. Remember it, while I'm riding you in this chair. Picture it, as you're coming hard and deep inside me."

Holy. Shit.

I did my best. I imagined my beautiful woman in that sexy lingerie as she straddled me and did exactly what she said she would, riding me with her hands clutched around my neck, and her cries resounding throughout the room. We put 18th century French furniture craftsmanship to the test, as I don't think I'd ever experienced sex like that in my life. Mind-blowing. Love and lust, in perfect, equal parts.

But I couldn't admit to her that I didn't think twice about what she wore. It didn't even register. Charlotte would never know—as I couldn't ever quite explain it—that when she and I made love, there was nothing else in my black world but the sensation of her.

When it Rains...

⠟⠓⠑⠝ ⠊⠞ ⠗⠁⠊⠝⠎ ⠄ ⠄ ⠄

The big day arrived. Ava couldn't miss too much work so she flew back to London. She said goodbye to me with a hug, a kiss, and a whispered "good luck," and then it was nearly time.

"I'm going to miss her," Charlotte sighed, as we took a cab back to our hotel. "So. What should we do? I have all day before the show."

I told her I'd planned a picnic on the grassy expanse below the Eiffel Tower, and she was delighted. But she made a lamenting sound when we stepped out of the hotel.

"It's cloudy," she said "Looks like rain."

My heart sank, and I hefted the basket hanging off my right arm. "How bad is it?"

"Not bad. Oh, there's a patch of blue! We should be okay."

I nodded. Jesus, had I ever been this nervous in my entire life? I doubted it. Not even the first time I base-jumped were my guts this twisted into knots. I was glad for my sunglasses, hid behind them, as we took a taxi to the Eiffel Tower.

There, we set up our picnic, and Charlotte described to me the immense tower over us, and the heavy sky beyond. Then she played right into my nervous, twitching hands.

"This reminds me of our first picnic in Central Park. Do you remember? It was the day after that really bad migraine." She sidled up close to me on the blanket. "You kissed me that night. Our first kiss. That's when I knew I was falling madly in love with you. That kiss…"

She laid her lips to mine, and my jangling nerved calmed down. This was Charlotte, after all. And the love I had for her soothed my anxiety away.

"I fell for you that night, too," I told her. "You were the only thing sweet and good in my miserable world."

"And you were bringing my music back to life, Noah. Little by little." She smiled against my lips. "But then on that picnic, you told me you couldn't kiss me again."

"Yes, I had a fabulous habit of saying the exact opposite of what I really felt."

"Oh yeah? You wanted to kiss me then too?" Her voice was soft and warm, and so full of love.

"Yeah, baby. I wanted to kiss you with the warm sunlight on my face, and the fresh air that I'd been locked away from, and kiss you. And never stop." I turned toward her, one hand reaching around behind me to my jacket where the little velvet box lay. "I don't ever want to stop kissing you, Charlotte. Every day, every hour of my life, I want to be with you."

The first drops of rain began to fall, but I hardly felt them.

She took off my sunglass and ran the tips of her fingers down my cheeks. "Kiss me now," she whispered, and I did, utterly swept away by her. Her mouth, her lips, the velvet of her little tongue...

And then a *boom* shook the air so loudly I felt it in my chest. The sky broke open and the rain came down in sheets, as if a dam had burst.

Charlotte shrieked in real fear, and I couldn't blame her. Lightning was probably crackling over the sky and we were sitting under the world's biggest lightning rod.

We scrambled to our feet, and gathered as much of our ruined picnic as we could, and Charlotte led me across a street, under the shelter of an awning.

"Oh my god, that scared the hell out of me," Charlotte laughed nervously. "And we're soaked. I wonder how hard it will be to find a taxi...?" She put her hand on my arm. "Hey. You okay? I'm sorry the rain ruined your picnic, honey. But I loved every minute. Even if we only had a few."

I nodded. God, she was so generous. And so full of love. Maybe I could salvage something. A proposal in the Paris rain. But this rain wasn't romantic. It was icy and cold, and Charlotte was already shivering.

We went back to the hotel and took a hot bath together, which soothed my frustration and disappointment, but not by much.

I sat down that night to work on my book. A book that still didn't have an ending.

Peru
⠏⠑⠗⠥

Charlotte's mini-tour took us to Sao Paolo, Brazil, and from there, she took me to Peru for my birthday. There, on the Huayna Picchu, she played the dawn, painting it in vibrant color with her violin, describing it with the music that lived in her soul.

I should have brought the ring. I should have asked her right then, as I kissed her lips and held her in my trembling arms. But whatever pain and bitterness that might have been lingering in my heart since the accident, was gone, and left no room for regret.

We went back to the hotel in Sacred Valley, and I made love to her with my entire heart and soul guiding my movements. I gave her everything I had, and I felt her do the same. Every breath she exhaled, every moan and cry, every touch of her fingers over my skin and my scars, my name on her lips…she gave it all to me. We were immersed in each other. The pleasure that came at the end was just an added reward.

She slept after, as we'd awoken early to be on the top of Huayuna before dawn, and I mentally readied myself to propose to her when she awoke. It might not have been a grand gesture—but after the extraordinary gift she'd given me up on that mountain, I was ready. I couldn't feel more complete than I did that morning, and Charlotte agreeing to be my wife would put me over the edge.

I dozed beside her, a silly grin lingering on my face…that soon morphed into a grimace of pain. I scrambled to the bathroom, took an Azapram, and slumped down against the bathroom wall to wait out the migraine that came over me like a tsunami, praying Charlotte wouldn't wake.

But she did.

"What's happening? Noah…"

"I'm okay," I said, the croak in my voice making the lie obvious. "Had a migraine but it's going away. Go back to sleep, baby. I'll be in soon. It's…almost over. Almost…."

"Oh, honey." She knelt beside me and cradled my head to her chest. "Is it getting better? You took a pill?" She took the Azapram bottle out of my slack hand, and her chest beneath my cheek hitched with a gasp. "Noah…This bottle had seven pills last week. *Seven.* I know because I packed it before we left for Sao Paulo. You have only two left?"

"Charlotte…"

"Did you have *five* migraines in one week? Or maybe…Lucien told me these things were potent. Are you…addicted?" She sucked in a shaky breath. "Noah, what's going on?"

Her fear and worry were awful to hear, which is precisely why I tried to keep this from her in the first place.

"I'm not addicted to the pills," I said as the pain drummed a heavy, hard beat in the back of my skull. "Or maybe I am. Maybe they're not working anymore…"

"How long have they been this bad? This frequent?" Charlotte's hands buffered my face, forcing me to look at her if I could. "Noah, *why didn't you tell me*?"

"I didn't want to scare you."

Or me. Now that she knew, the fear that something was really wrong with me ballooned up; as if admitting it out loud gave it power.

"It's nothing," I said, trying to take it all back. "I've been stressed, tired. It's not worth worrying about."

But of course, Charlotte was having none of that.

"You don't do that, Noah," she said, her voice tremulous but firm too. "*We* don't do that. We don't *spare* each other anything."

"I'm *fine*," I said, turning my head away.

"No," she said, her voice cracking. "You're not. And I've been too busy flying around on my tour to really see that you aren't. Oh my god, how could I not see…?"

Her guilt was like a whip, flaying me. Another reason I'd kept it hidden.

"Because there's nothing to see, Charlotte. Please do not take this on yourself. The drugs aren't working. A resistance or something. That's all."

"Okay, fine." She sniffled. "Is that all it is? Good. Then lets get you home to a doctor and she can change your prescription. Give you better medicine. But you can't just keep suffering—"

"I can't go back," I said, my frustration with this whole mess beating the migraine pain. "I did not crack my head open, or almost lose my leg, or bust my ass in physical therapy…I didn't just stumble around Europe blind so I could wind up back in…" I bit off the words, shaking my head.

"Back where?" she breathed. "A hospital? Is that were you think you need to go?"

"God, I'm just scaring the hell out of you which is why I didn't

103

want to say anything." I stood up on shaking legs and felt my way past her, back to the bedroom. I picked up a pillow from the bed to lay against. Instead I threw it back down. "I just...I thought I was done, that's all. Done with being scared and in pain, with the smell of death hanging all over me." I shook my head. "It's fine. *I'm* fine. I'll see a doctor. Get a better prescription, but I don't want to talk about it anymore. I just need a little sleep."

I crawled into bed to try to salvage something of the morning, trying not to think of yet another proposal ruined, or how Charlotte wasn't the only one who was fucking scared.

The migraine was receding, but I could feel Charlotte's presence, the warm energy of her, as she stood regarding me.

Finally, I felt her slide into bed beside me. Wordlessly, she sidled up close, wrapped me in her legs and arms, and pulled me to her so that my head was pillowed against her breast. She stroked my hair gently, massaging the last of the pain away. I tensed at first...then sighed and melted against her.

"I'm sorry, baby...So sorry."

"Sssshh, no." She kissed my temple. "How long?"

"I don't know. Since Rome, I think. So that was..."

"Early July," she said, swallowing hard. "Almost four months, Noah."

"Yeah. I was stressed, baby. That's all."

I felt her shake her head. "We're going home. Back to New York City. Tomorrow."

"Damn. You've worked so hard to plan this trip for us..."

"Doesn't matter. You're the only thing that matters. We're done traveling for a while. And you are going straight to a doctor."

I squeezed my eyes shut in defeat. *I blew it. My chance to ask her, ruined. And now she's scared.*

"Sleep now, Noah. Get some sleep." She kissed me again, held me close, and I felt enveloped by her, by her body and her love, and I nestled closer.

"We're going home."

Return to New York

Back in New York City. The townhouse. It sounded and smelled the same as when I'd left it, eons ago, but felt different now. Charlotte was back, and so the place felt like a home instead of the black prison I'd locked myself up in after the accident.

We had an appointment with my old neurologist at Lenox Hill the following morning. On the phone he'd sounded concerned. It leaked out from behind his professional words when it wasn't supposed to, and then fear settled into my chest like a lead weight. Roaring, relentless migraines. Dizziness. Nausea. I didn't have to be a Google M.D. for my mind to jump to the worst conclusion.

"Come to bed," Charlotte called to me that first night. "Get some rest. You can pick that up again later."

I was writing. Writing these words. Speaking them into the machine where they vanished from me, but were written down too, so that others can read them. So Charlotte can finally read them, and know what she means to me. I could speak until I was hoarse and I'd never run out of ways to tell her how much I loved her, but right then, on the brink of an unknown tomorrow, I struggled to find the *right* words, to lock them in place for all time.

"Charlotte," I finally whispered into the machine. "Thank you. Thank you for loving me like you do."

The next morning, we called a cab to take me to my neurologist's office at Lenox Hill. While we were standing on the curb outside the townhouse, waiting for the taxi, the ground slid out from under me. My hand slipped off Charlotte's arm, and I stumbled sideways, to land hard on my knees. And still, the ground beneath my hands tried to slip away.

A rushing sound filled my ears, and Charlotte's voice came from a great distance, as did the sound of a car engine. Hands lifted me, softer hands held me, and then the pervasive blackness dropped down over my thoughts too, and I knew nothing…

An old terror grabbed hold of me with both hands and shook me awake. The smells—cleanser and latex—filled my nose. The beeping machines and monitors, the voices and footsteps in the hall outside, echoed in my ears.

It all came flooding back. The accident. My head and neck were weighted down, metal plated and heavy, and it was so fucking dark. I was anchored to the bed and grabbing at my eyes for the bandages that weren't there, before begging, in a voice torn ragged with terror, for someone to turn the lights back on. Please. Why is it so dark? Why…?

I sucked in a breath and bolted upright. Not anchored down. No pain. In the dark, yes, but then memory, such as it is to me now, came back. A hand slipped into mine.

Charlotte. This wasn't after the accident, this was new. New and yet frighteningly similar to my remaining senses.

A barrage of tests, worried family members, and more tests, marked that first day and Charlotte tried to get me through these hours in which we waited for the doctors to tell us what the hell was wrong with me. I was scared, but I hated that Charlotte was scared more.

I slept with her standing guard over me and awoke again, to hear her crying. I heard her sniffle, and smelled the salt of her tears.

"Hey," I murmured, reaching for her hand. "What's wrong? Why are you crying, baby?"

I wondered if the doctor had pulled Charlotte aside and told her, yes, we can explain the increased migraines and dizziness, and we're so sorry…

"I'm crying because I'm mad at you, Noah! And mad at myself. For being so ignorant to how exhausted you really are. How hard it's been for you…" She huffed a sigh. "I read your book tonight."

"That bad, huh?" I teased but she wasn't hearing it.

"I read about Europe and I just can't believe what you did for me. What you did for *us*. To undertake something like that, blind and alone…And it was so dangerous, and lonely, and exhausting…God, Noah."

She crumpled into sobs and I held my arms out to her. "Come here, baby."

Charlotte crawled back into bed with me, face to face. I wiped her tears away but more fell.

"I couldn't tell you, Charlotte, and I didn't want to," I said, stroking her hair. "It's not what was important."

She lifted her head. "It's important to me! When I think—I mean, *really* think—how it was for you…It's astonishing, and I feel like such an idiot. That first night, in Salzburg, you told me about your trip, but I didn't listen. I heard but I didn't listen. I was too happy to see you, and you...you hardly described it at all."

"On purpose," I said.

"But why?"

"Because, Charlotte, I'd have felt like I was taking advantage of you. I had to leave you, and that was fucking awful. But I didn't want you to forgive me just because the trip was hard. I wanted you to forgive me because it was the right thing to do. Charlotte..." I held her sweet face in my hands. "It was my trial by fire. I don't need to tell you how badly it burned. It doesn't matter. What matters is that you know you're worth it. I'd do it again a hundred times over if I had to. For you."

"You don't have to, Noah," she whispered. "You don't have to work so *hard*. And, my god, there is absolutely *nothing* to forgive. Don't you know how much you have given me? Even before my tour started? Noah, the tour *only happened* because of you. Your love and belief in me brought my music back to life."

"You would have found it without me, baby."

"*No*. When? After another year of scraping by? Another year of lackluster practices, and skipped auditions?" Her hands tightened their hold on mine. "You were the one who got me to really look at what was slipping away. You caught it and held it out to me, and said, 'Take it, it's yours. Now is your time.' And I had to go and dig it out of myself. I had to do it alone the same way you had to cope with your blindness alone. Only I wasn't strong enough to leave you. But *you* were strong enough. Strong and brave."

"I didn't feel brave," I murmured against her hair. "I wanted to quit every day. Every minute."

"But you didn't," she said. "I'm so grateful to you for doing the right thing for both of us, no matter how hard." She burrowed against me tighter. "You are brave, Noah. So brave..."

I held her and kissed her until her hitching breaths became even. I thought she might have fallen asleep, but she sniffled and pulled away to settle herself on the pillow facing me.

"Do you have it with you?" she asked.

"Have what with me?"

"The ring."

I opened my mouth, then snapped it shut again. "You read about Paris."

"I read everything."

"Then you know I kept trying to find the right moment and couldn't."

"Right now," she said softly. "Right now is the right moment."

I scoffed. "God, no. Here? That would be the least romantic proposal in the history of matrimony."

"That's why it's perfect," she insisted. "No grand gestures. If you asked me what my dream proposal would be, it's just you and me, anywhere, starting the rest of our lives together."

God, this woman. I wanted to jump in with both feet, and do whatever she asked. To ask *her*, finally, the only question left between us. But the sound of my own pulse came back to me on a machine, reminding me of exactly where we were and what it could mean.

"The doctors are going to come in this room any minute now and God knows what they're going to say. It feels selfish."

"Be selfish, then. For once, be selfish, Noah."

"And if it's bad news? What do we do then?"

"We get married." I felt her soft hands on my jaw. "I'm yours, Noah. In sickness and in health, and nothing is going to change that. *Nothing*."

Warmth flooded me, driving back the hospital cold and my fear and doubts. I kissed her fiercely, and held her face after, my eyes searching, then relenting. Charlotte was there, on the side of the black, and she always would be.

"Jacket pocket. Left side."

She slipped off the bed and returned quickly. She climbed back into that narrow old hospital bed with me, and pressed the small black velvet box into my hand.

"You read the book. You already know what it looks like," I muttered, turning the box over and over.

"I have an idea. That's not the same as reality."

I nodded and opened the box. Her sharp intake of breath sounded reassuring and goddamn, I was suddenly a nervous wreck.

"I didn't think you'd want something flashy," I said. "And it's old as hell, which I thought you'd appreciate." I cleared my throat. "So…uh, do you like it?

"Oh, Noah. It's the most beautiful thing I've ever seen."

"It felt like the right one…for you."

I felt for the ring and pulled it from the box, and the hospital fell away: the beeping machines, the sterile air, the tubes and wires. It's just Charlotte and me in this moment, because she was absolutely right. This was the time and place, however improbable it seemed.

We were sharing my pillow, face to face, and I inched closer. "Come here." I pulled her to me and pressed my forehead to hers. "I want to ask you something, baby, and I want to look you in the eye when I do it."

Our foreheads together, I closed my eyes, and when I opened them, I knew I was looking right at her. My eyes met hers precisely, because I felt her body react, her breath catching.

Without breaking contact, I find her left hand and take it. "I love you, Charlotte. You've given me everything. You showed me I could walk the earth alone, in the dark, but I don't want to. I want you by my side, now and forever." I sucked in a breath, my heart pounding like a sledgehammer. *My Charlotte...* "Will you marry me?"

"Yes, Noah," she whispered, and her voice is filled with happy tears. "Of course, yes. Yes."

I slipped the ring onto her finger, and kissed her, and of all the thousands of kisses between us, none were as sweet or good as that one.

After, I pulled her into my arms and held her, vowing that if the doctor had bad news, I'd fight as hard as I needed to. As hard as I did the first time when the rocks broke me. And I wasn't afraid. I took hold of that perfect moment, of the feel of that extraordinary woman in my arms, and let it in, to keep it for all time.

It was astonishing to me that I could know this much happiness. Even amid the unknown, I felt it and understood it for what it was. It's the sunrise I saw with my eyes in Peru, and the sunrise I saw in my heart with Charlotte's music to paint it for me. It is the endless possibility of life. Pain seems inevitable. Or expected. We accept it, I think, as something unavoidable, and happiness is a gift hanging just out of reach; a privilege only a few of us are lucky enough to have.

But it's not. It's right there, all around us, if we just have the courage to reach our hands into the dark, and take it.

Take it. Hold on. And never let go.

Epilogue

Charlotte, three years later

I walked down the corridors of NYU's Liberal Arts college building, though *waddled* is probably more accurate. I looked—and felt—like I'd swallowed a bowling ball. *I'm too short to be this pregnant*, I thought. And I still had twelve weeks to go. The mere idea that I was going to get even bigger was too exhausting to contemplate.

I stopped at the bench outside Noah's office and gratefully lowered myself onto it. A clock on the wood-paneled wall opposite said I had ten minutes until his class got out. I eased a sigh, my hand running absently over my rounded belly. The baby stirred and I smiled. I smiled wider. I hadn't stopped smiling all day, and I itched to take out the smallish box that lay snug in my bag, to look at its contents for the hundredth time that day. But I left it alone and closed my eyes, just for a minute...

And promptly dozed off.

I awoke with a jolt as the hall filled with the echoing voices and footsteps of dozens of students. Amid the crowd, I saw Noah, holding the arm of a colleague and coming my way; sunglasses on, white stick tapping from side to side.

My heart clanged madly just from the sight of my gorgeous husband. I silently thanked the NYU dress code that even guest instructors were required to wear a suit. Today, Noah wore light gray—my favorite on him—with a cobalt tie and gold paisley print. He looked devastating, and I could tell by the stolen glances from some of the female students that I wasn't alone in that estimation.

The professor who guided him—Harry Albright, if I remembered correctly—saw me, and smiled brightly beneath salt-and-pepper mustaches. He spoke a few words to Noah, informing him I was here, I guessed. The way Noah's face lit up was like a jolt of pure happiness straight to my heart.

"We've arrived at your office," Harry Albright said as they approached, "where your wife awaits, as promised. Charlotte, you look radiant."

"Thank you, Harry. I don't feel radiant. I feel like a walrus."

"A walrus? Yesterday it was a manatee." Noah let go of Harry's arm, and reached out his hand to me. "Pace yourself, baby. We still have three months to go and you're going to run out of bloated sea animals to compare yourself to."

"Oh, aren't you hilarious," I said, as Noah planted a soft kiss on my cheek, his hand going at once to my stomach. He always greeted us both at the same time.

"I can say that," Noah told Harry, "because it's utter horseshit. She's gorgeous and that's a fact."

"Indeed she is," Harry said, with a twinkle in his eye. "And Charlotte, are you welcoming a boy or a girl?"

"Girl," Noah said automatically, infusing that one syllable with fierce pride and love. "We're having a girl."

Harry laughed. "Of course you are, Mr. Lake! You tell me and the rest of the department approximately sixteen times a day." He turned and winked at me. "First-time proud father syndrome. Textbook."

"Don't you have an appointment, Harry?" Noah inquired, a small smile twitching his lips.

"Indeed. Charlotte, so good to see you, and congratulations again on your…what was it? Ah yes, a girl."

With a wink for me, Harry rejoined the current of students flowing down the hallway. Some were likely Noah's own students who took his Comparative Literature course: Writing Memory. He was a guest professor for the year—the success of his memoir allowing for that—but I think he liked teaching more than he realized. I think he liked it enough to make it a career. For a little while anyway. I couldn't imagine he'd stick to one path for too long; he had too much wanderlust in him. We both did. We'd been traveling for the last year almost nonstop, until a little pink plus sign on a pregnancy test six months ago put the brakes on our travels.

"If we have to stop," Noah said when I told him the news, "then this is the best possible reason."

Now, he kissed me again, beaming like the proud father Harry described him to be. "This is a nice surprise. What are you doing here, babe?" His smile faltered. "Are you okay? The baby's okay…?"

"Everyone's perfectly fine," I said gently.

I never laughed off his worry. It was hard enough, I thought, to be an expectant parent. Even harder, when you had to travel that uncertain road in the dark.

Noah's concerned frown lifted back into a smile, his hand gentle on my stomach over my flowered dress. The baby kicked or rolled or did whatever baby gymnasts do: punching my ribs and stomping my bladder at the same time.

"She's awake," Noah said quietly, a soft, sweet smile on his face I'm sure no one ever saw but me.

"You can say that again," I laughed, wincing. "She hasn't stopped moving all day. I was thinking you and I could take a walk, get her settled down. You're done for the day, right?"

"I am," Noah said. "Let me grab my stuff and we're outta here."

He unlocked the door behind me, and I watched him, my own fierce pride burning in my heart, as he made his way around his office with ease. It was dim—he never bothered with lights unless he had students. He gathered his Braille keyboard and laptop, and stuffed them into his bag, along with the latest book he was reading: a wide, thick novel printed in Braille. He'd studied hard at the Helen Keller Foundation, and in nine months was opening real books again, and I know it was like a whole new world opened up to him. I'd never been so proud.

We stepped back into the hall that was quieter now, though not by much. A student passed, gave my swollen belly a second take, and shouted, "Oooh! Way to go, Mr. Lake!"

I laughed while Noah pretended to be irritated, when I could see he was proud too.

I was fine with taking the subway but Noah wouldn't hear of it. He didn't like the crowds or the idea of someone bumping into me or harassing me, and him not being able to prevent it. His protectiveness was sweet but intense too. After the mugging where I'd lost my violin, and then Deacon in the elevator all those years ago, Noah had made a vow to keep me safe as best he could. Maybe I was supposed to feel affronted by that—Melanie or Ava might think so—but I just felt loved. And cherished. And safe. I always felt safe with Noah.

We took a cab to what was now our townhouse.

At our wedding three years ago we'd insisted that in lieu of gifts, guests make a donation to the American Cancer Society. In the hospital, Noah had received the best news about his migraines and dizzy spells: a severe reaction to the very medication designed to ease them. His meds were switched, and since then he'd only had a handful of serious headaches, and no more dizziness. We'd been blessed beyond anything we could have hoped. But all over the hospital—all over the country— other patients weren't hearing the same good news.

Noah's parents, however, couldn't help but do something big. Our wedding had been a beautiful event in Bozeman, Montana, in a tiny little chapel overlooking the Gallatin Valley. Small and simple—but elegant too—with just our closest family and friends. It was perfect, and I thought I couldn't be any happier.

But when we returned to New York, my new father-in-law pressed a key and a deed into Noah's hand, and told us the townhouse was ours now, and he wouldn't take no for an answer. Then my joy overflowed, and I knew exactly why. The townhouse was where my life restarted. Where my *heart* restarted; brought back to life by Noah's resuscitative kiss. I couldn't imagine staying in New York City and not living there.

I thought Noah would feel strange or uncomfortable, given all of those long, solitary months he'd spent holed up there. But he told me he was glad. With me there, he said, it felt different. It felt like home. Any lingering demons were cast out when we redecorated to better suit his blindness and our tastes, and then we spent the two weeks of our at-home honeymoon christening the hell out of every room in the house.

That helped a lot too.

Now, I waited in the foyer on the first floor as Noah changed out of his suit and into his usual athletic pants and t-shirt. I looked toward what had been my room when I was an employee here. It was now the guest room. The guest room on the third floor was now the baby's room.

The baby's room.

I smiled, and hefted my bag that held the small box I'd been given today. I kept the bag on my left side, which was awkward to me, but I didn't want Noah to feel it and wonder why I'd brought it along on our walk. He'd know soon enough.

He came down the stairs two at a time, and I just…watched.

He was so tall. So damn tall and sexy; he never failed to take my breath away, even after three and half years of drinking him in every day.

I'd hoped I'd always feel this way.

I knew I always would.

Noah felt my gaze on him. As usual. "Got something in my teeth?"

"No. It's just…you."

He grinned crookedly and bent down to kiss me. And not a light, shallow peck, either. A deep, intense kiss that I felt in my lower belly that still burned for him, baby on board or not. Noah never kissed me like I was a delicate, fragile pregnant woman. Never.

"Where are we headed?" he asked, unfolding his white stick. "Just a walk? Don't you need to rest up for your recording session tomorrow?"

"I canceled it," I said, leading him out in the beautiful New York City spring twilight. "Or postponed it, I should say. I warned them that might be the case. Paganini's Caprice is insane, and I just can't get the movement I need." I glanced down fondly at my belly. "Just one of many schedule interruptions or changes this little bugger is going to impose on us."

Noah made a noncommittal sound, his expression darkening. I knew he was thinking about all the other things a baby requires, and of his deep-rooted fear he wouldn't be able to provide them. Or worse, that his blindness would hurt her somehow, or put her in danger. I couldn't insult his intelligence and deny we had challenges, but I also hadn't the faintest doubt he'd be nothing short of wonderful with our baby.

We crossed the always-busy Columbus Avenue, and then started up the short path to what I considered 'our bench.' I tucked my bag on my left side and let out a gusty sigh of relief to be off my feet.

"I remember this bench," Noah said, stretching out, and setting his white stick aside. He turned my direction. "Feeling nostalgic?"

"Something like that," I said, biting back a smile. "Do you remember what happened here?"

His face softened. "As if I could forget. This is where I looked at you for the first time."

"Yes. And you told me that you couldn't see anything. But that wasn't true, was it?"

"No," he replied. "I saw you. You were so beautiful. I hadn't expected that…or what I felt, seeing you. I didn't expect that either."

"Oh? You felt something for me? Even then?" I teased lightly. "I seem to recall a very decisive, 'I can't see shit with my hands.'"

"I may have been prone to exaggeration," he said with a cough.

"I thought so." I snuggled up against him, and he put his arm around me. "But you said you hadn't expected to feel what you did. And what was that, may I ask three years later?"

114

Noah turned his sightless gaze forward for a moment, as if trying to put his thoughts to words.

"You're radiant, Charlotte. They said that about you on our wedding day, and now again that you're pregnant, but you've always been radiant. And the first time I saw that beauty under my hands, I felt how I feel when opening a brand new book. Do you know how that is? Where you only need to read the first few pages and you're already thinking, 'This might be a good one. One of the best ones. One of the rare finds that stays with you forever.'"

He turned to me, a small, soft smile on his lips.

"That's how I felt, but I was far too bottled up and ready to explode to ever say something like that."

"Oh," I breathed, my heart pounding as if we were on a first date instead of married three years and expecting a child. "Oh, Noah." I sniffed and brushed away tears.

Thanks to my hormones I cried at the drop of a hat but these tears weren't hormonal. I didn't expect Noah to keep sweeping me off my feet, but somehow he always managed to do it.

He turned to face me, and took his sunglasses off, his hazel eyes sweeping over me. I didn't say a word but leaned close to my husband and let him find me with his lips. He kissed me slowly, a deep pull of his mouth on mine, before breaking off gently to brush a stray hair from my cheek.

I caught and held his hand. "What do I look like now?"

He touched my eyes, my cheeks, my lips, gently feeling the contours of my face.

"You look...happy," he whispered.

"Yes," I breathed, "that's exactly what I am. I love you, and I'm so happy with you. And...I have something for you."

"Oh, yeah?"

"Yeah." I bit my lip, excitement for my surprise ballooning in my chest. "Before your accident, did you ever see one of those 3D ultrasounds they can do now? Instead of grainy black and white, you can really see the contours and details of the baby's face. It's amazing."

Noah nodded. "I think I remember seeing something like that. A long time ago," he said dully. "Did you want one? We can search around for a place that does them."

He sounded casual but his fingers drummed the back of the bench, and my heart ached a little. It hurt him that he couldn't see his baby growing inside me. At our regular ultrasound appointment, Noah had clutched my hand and asked the tech over and over, "How does she look?" He was concerned for the baby's health first and foremost, but I knew too, he felt blocked from the special moment. He couldn't see what the tech, my doctor, and I could all see—his baby in my womb, wiggling and kicking, her heart beating fast and strong. It broke my heart.

Which is why, earlier that day, I'd gone back for another.

"Well, I already found a place that does that and I had a new ultrasound done."

"And she's okay, right?" he asked, automatically tense with worry. "Everything looks good?"

"Yes, honey," I said soothingly. "She's perfect. And beautiful. The pictures were quite stunning. So vivid. This place had the latest equipment…even one of those new 3D printers." I reached into my bag and pulled out the square white box and opened it. I took out the cast—a square of plaster—and pressed it to Noah's hand. My voice fell to a whisper. "It's amazing what they can do with technology these days."

"What…?"

I watched, my heart in my throat, as he trailed his long fingers over the cast, investigating. He stopped at the center with a small gasp, and his hand began to tremble. He found the curve of a tiny, chubby cheek, then a dimpled little chin, and two eyes squeezed shut tight.

"Is that…?" He cleared his throat and tried again. "Is that my baby?"

My eyes blurred with tears to see his. I leaned close, kissed his ear, his cheek. "That's your baby."

He moved his fingertips over her again, and again. "I can see her. This is her. Our baby…"

He sat very still for a moment, but for his fingers that looked at his daughter because his eyes could not. A strangled sound erupted from deep in his chest, and he bent over his knees, one hand covering his eyes, the other holding the 3D print. I held his shoulders as they shook, and snuggled close to kiss neck, my tears falling on the shoulder of his shirt.

"God, Charlotte," he said hoarsely, and then pulled me close, his lips brushing against my hair. "Thank—"

"No." I shook my head, cutting him off before he could thank me for what was already his. "She is our baby, Noah. Yours and mine. We made her together. This…" I touched the print. "This is just what you deserve. As her father. And I know you are going to be an amazing father."

He nodded, wiped his eyes on the crook of his sleeve, chagrined at his loss of control. "I'll do my best."

His best. This from a man who spent six weeks traveling across Europe blind for me. For us. Noah's *best* meant his heart and soul, blood and guts, sweat and tears, and my heart was filled with so much love for him, I could hardly contain it.

"She looks just like you," Noah said, still looking at the baby.

"Mm, she has your chin, and God, do I hope she has your eyes."

"My eyes," Noah murmured.

He didn't finish his thought and I didn't ask. Noah pulled me to him, holding the 3D print tight in one hand—as if he'd never put it down—and rested his other on my stomach. We listened to New York all around us, and felt our baby move beneath our hands.

It felt like it had always been this way, he and I, together. Amazing to think there'd been a time when we weren't. We traveled so far to get here—across continents and great stretches of the black unknown.

I thought of the angry, bitter man who'd holed himself up in one room, listening to someone else read, and the heartbroken young woman who'd just needed a decent job and a little bit of peace. We'd both been smashed up by life and rearranged until neither of us knew ourselves. But somehow we'd found each other, helped each other put our broken pieces back together to make something new and whole. And something even more than that. I rubbed my rounded belly and smiled. We'd started with a maybe, and that maybe turned into a miracle.

The last caramel-colored light began to slip away, and we rose from our bench. Noah's hand found the crook of my arm without having to reach, and I sighed to feel his strong grip there. Everything was where it was supposed to be.

"Come on, baby," Noah said, bending to kiss me. "Let's go home."

End

Thank you for reading. I always love to hear from my readers. Please visit me on Facebook or Twitter @EmmaS_writes

Here is a sneak peak at the next novel in the City Lights series, coming February 2016

Beside You in the Moonlight
City Lights Book IV: Paris

Janey
September, 1970
Paris, France

I dream of Danny every night.

A little sliver of a dream and nothing more. Always the same. He is standing in my family's vineyard, and the rows of grape trees—each perfectly cut, evenly spaced—roll across the land, curving and climbing up the mountain behind him. It's always twilight, just before the sun slips below the horizon completely. Gold hues, bruised with purple and blue, paint the sky above Danny. He wears his army fatigues and his helmet; a battered pack of cigarettes is tucked into the band. There is an M-16 is strapped to his shoulder, and he carries it as if he were born with it, though he'd never touched one before the war. His sleeves are rolled up to reveal grimy, sweat-and-blood covered arms, and his boots are caked with mud. It's as if he's stepped out the jungle to be here. His smile is sweet but there are infinities of sadness behind his eyes as he raises a hand to me in farewell. He never says anything, but for that silent goodbye, but I don't tell him goodbye in return.

Come back to me…

That is the only thought that lives in my heart and Danny's hand drops wearily, and I know I will see him again tomorrow night.